PATRIOTS' CALL

A "DC Seven" Thriller

Carl R. Baker

Published by Hallard Press LLC.
www.HallardPress.com   Info@HallardPress.com   352-234-6099
Bulk copies of this book can be ordered at Info@HallardPress.com

Publisher's Cataloging-in-Publication data

Names: Baker, Carl R., author.
Title: Patriots' Call: a "DC Seven" thriller / Carl R. Baker.
Description: The Villages, FL: Hallard Press, 2022.
Identifiers: LCCN: 2022917312 | ISBN: 978-1-951188-65-8 (paperback) | 978-1-951188-66-5 (ebook)
Subjects: LCSH Presidents--Fiction. | Political corruption--Fiction. | Politics and government--United States--Fiction. | Political fiction. | Thriller fiction. | BISAC FICTION / Political | FICTION / Thrillers / Political
Classification: LCC PS3602.A5852 E64 2022 | DDC 813.6--dc23

Printed in the United States of America.   1

ISBN: 978-1-951188-65-8 (Paperback)
ISBN: 978-1-951188-66-5 (EBook)

EVIL IS POWERLESS IF THE GOOD ARE UNAFRAID.
—RONALD REAGAN

DISCLAIMER

The conclusions and opinions expressed in this book
are those of the author unless otherwise stated.

While the reader of this novel may recognize
that some of the incidents outlined in the book are true,
this book is a work of fiction.

DEDICATION

This book is dedicated to those who serve or have served in the military or law enforcement and stayed loyal to their oath in their search for the truth. These are challenging times for all of us. And although it seems like the world has gone crazy, know that you have the support of the majority of the people you serve, and you have the armor of our loving God for protection.

Other books by Carl R. Baker

BROKEN SUNSHINE
*A Case Study of Elder Abuse
and Exploitation in Florida*

ENEMIES IN THE WEST WING
A "DC Seven" Thriller

"The secret of freedom lies in the education of people, whereas the secret of tyranny is in keeping them ignorant."
—Maximilien Robespierre

INTRODUCTION

There is one fact upon which all Americans can agree. We are a nation that is horribly divided. Have you ever taken the time to determine why we are so split? Some believe that we are divided along political party lines, Democrats versus Republicans, or philosophical lines, liberals versus conservatives, or by government structure desires, socialists versus Constitutionalists, or by region, the north versus the south or the east coast versus the west coast, or by skin color, white versus black and brown. Believe it or not, none of these groupings are individually or collectively responsible for our country's division. It is something much simpler.

Truth is what divides our country, those who choose to seek the truth versus those who choose to hide the truth, those who tell the truth versus those who do not, those who accept the truth versus those who deny it. And there are examples everywhere: the media, the governments throughout the world, the corporate world, the universities, the scientific/research industry and others.

Determining what is true and real has become impossible due to the internet and other social media sites that have surged in the last few years. Biased fact checkers and subjective algorithms have only made it worse. There is no universal standard for the truth. Politicians lie to the public daily. It is against the law to lie to Congress or the FBI. Yet they can lie to us with impunity.

If the truth truly sets us free, we are all imprisoned.

This book is a sequel to my earlier book, TO DEFEND AGAINST ALL ENEMIES – Foreign and Domestic, which I wrote twelve years ago. Due to circumstances beyond my control, the book has been republished under a different title: ***Enemies in the West Wing.*** The characters are now also twelve years older and again concerned about the future of America.

This is a fact-based, fictional story which gives the reader a true understanding of the growing problems our country is facing. The statistics and the discussions during the Zoom meetings are as accurate as the articles you read in today's newspapers.

I want to thank the readers for their concern for our country. The truth is the first step in saving America. I also want to thank those who supported me and took the time to review my manuscript: my wife, Katherine who I relied on much more than she realized; my brother Bruce and Dr. Teri Melton, who has been a life-long friend and has reviewed each book I have written.

To John Prince and Nancy Hellekson at Hallard Press, thank you for your suggestions and working so close with me. You are outstanding at what you do, and I have gained two good friends.

"*The Constitution is not a document for the government to restrain the people; it is an instrument for the people to restrain the government.*"
    —Patrick Henry

Some Americans will never appreciate America until after they have helped destroy it and have then begun to suffer the consequences.
　—Thomas Sowell

CHAPTER 1

I looked at my cell phone and saw that Jim Bruce was calling. I answered, "Good morning, Jim."

Jim began, "I wish it were a good morning, Chuck. America has had over ten years of prosperity since the Sanchez fiasco. Not in my worst nightmare, did I ever think we would have a year like 2021 in America and 2022 does not look any better. America is in deep trouble. Our monthly lunch on Wednesday will be two hours rather than one. Please let everyone know; Tom has a doctor's appointment and won't be able to make it. See you Wednesday."

And that was the end of our conversation. I know Jim well enough to know three things; he just received news that was not good, he was in a rush, and whatever he wanted to tell me would have to be in person and not on a cell phone.

Now my mind was going in a hundred different directions. Not one of us in our group is satisfied with the events and decisions taking place in Washington and we were all shocked at the horrible screw-up on the withdrawal from Afghanistan. The inexcusable lack of law and order is a whole other issue. Anyone paying any attention to the news who has an IQ over eighty, knows there is a leadership void in the White House. It is obvious the President has cognitive issues and I certainly want him to do well. However, we do not know who is making all the decisions for the President, but we can see that the American way of life is declining rapidly. I guess we will be briefed at Wednesday's luncheon.

It has been over twelve years since President Sanchez committed suicide rather than facing impeachment. He chose death over the probability that he would spend the remainder of his life in federal prison. But Jim was right. Our country had recovered well from the corrupt Sanchez term in the Oval Office. But this Administration evidently has a social agenda and obviously has classified conservative Americans as their enemy.

Our group of seven has been together since the Sanchez investigation. The tragedies, the crimes, and the stress on our families and nation, all took a toll on us. But we survived, our families became stronger, and our friendship became a brotherhood. And the seven of us have had lunch together every month for twelve years. In addition, every year we have two large gatherings with all our families—one at Christmas and a picnic in June.

All of us are now retired from federal service. I was the Director of the Secret Service; Jim had retired as the Deputy Director of the FBI. John Walters retired as the Chief Judge of the United States Supreme Court; General John Monroe retired from the Army and his final position was in National Intelligence; Joe Wells retired from the CIA, as head of technology; Steve Mason retired as the United States Attorney General; and Tom Wilson retired as the Director of the FBI.

"Freedom from fear and injustice and oppression will be ours only in the measure that men who value such freedom are ready to sustain its possession."

—Dwight D. Eisenhower

CHAPTER 2

"No longer is the federal government concerned with what is best for America; that basic tenet has been replaced with the self-righteous elected federal officials' efforts to increase their own wealth and power so that they can retain their lifestyle and control this uninformed, deplorable population," I sarcastically stated to our group of patriots at our lunch meeting.

"I say this with a heavy heart when I reflect on all that happened twelve years ago. Greed has become a verb in Washington and with no real law and order, the United States of America is rapidly becoming a Banana Republic."

Jim Bruce added, "And that is why Chuck and I asked you to come here today. Based on our past experiences, we wanted your thoughts and concerns about the present direction of the country we love and spent our entire adult life protecting."

We all remember that 12:15 a.m. call we received on New Year's Day years ago. The FBI and WATCH24 agents were working a lead on the two dirty bombs possessed by the Mexican drug cartel. Information was that the bombs were moved in a U-Haul rental truck to be deployed at unknown locations in America. Sanchez henchman, Orlando Ortega and two other cartel members were killed in a shootout with the agents that morning in El Paso, Texas. And with their deaths, any leads that we had on the dirty bombs were buried with them.

Trace evidence confirmed that there was radioactive material in the truck, but that alone does not prove the presence of dirty bombs. We still have no idea where the bombs are located. It has been years since that day and our hope is that they have been dismantled or have deteriorated to the point of being useless. Unconfirmed information from the Mexican government is that the bombs have been updated, whatever that means, and now are in two different vehicles in the United States. We have no idea what the cartel may be targeting. What we do know is their original objective was to deploy them in the USA as a retaliation to the Sanchez case. Why is this resurfacing now? Because our country has open borders, a criminal justice system in chaos, a military which spends more time on Critical Race Theory than their defense mission, a weak President and Vice President, a majority in Congress that believes the populous is "deplorable" and the enemy to their socialistic agenda, and a corrupt federal government. For terrorists who want to destroy America, it does not get any better than this!

This is a meeting that none of us wanted, none of us anticipated, yet one that was necessary. America's tenure is certainly questionable if we continue down this path.

Twelve years ago, the six men in this room and Tom Wilson, came together to save our nation from what they considered an unconventional effort to centralize all power in the White House. When President Robert Sanchez's views and visions for America were in direct contrast with the populace, as well as circumventing the Constitution, we all knew we needed to stand up for America and take action.

Not one of us ever thought we would be in this position again and with the tragedies and stress all our families went through, there was no thought of ever repeating this. Yet here we are—experienced, twelve years older, apprehensive and worried about our country and families. However, we are all true patriots, and we know exactly what we must do.

We are a unique group of senior citizens from diverse backgrounds and work experience:

Everyone calls me Chuck, but my given name is Charles R. Burke and I retired six years ago as the Director of the Secret Service. I was the Special Agent-in-Charge of the White House Detail during the Sanchez Administration. The entire Sanchez investigation was difficult for my wife, Kim, and my two children, Tom and Marie. They all experienced much more than any husband and father would want to put them through, but they were strong. I have an amazing well- adjusted, patriotic, Christian family.

General John Paul Monroe was destined to be a soldier. He had decided at age ten that he wanted to go to West Point. He worked hard in high school and devoted all his free time to study and sports. He graduated third in his class with four high school letters for football, baseball, basketball and golf. He received an appointment to West Point in 1961 and graduated number two in his class. He and his high school sweetheart, Cindy, were married the next day.

He was a captain by the time he saw combat action in Vietnam. Shortly after beginning his tour, two infantry companies were pinned down by enemy fire and taking heavy casualties. Captain Monroe, who was in the adjacent sector with his infantry company, gathered as many resources as he could, including air support, and responded. After hours of intense fighting, the enemy retreated, and countless soldiers were saved. For their actions, the entire company received a Presidential Unit Citation and Captain Monroe received a Silver Star. That was only one of the events that defined General Monroe's military career which ended with four stars on his collar.

James W. Bruce was a retired Deputy Director of the Federal Bureau of Investigation and a close friend for over twenty years. He was known as the "go-to guy" in the FBI. With his knowledge, experience and network of associates, he could easily get the answer to your question or solve your problem. He was the epitome of a true professional. However, he is saddened to see the current corruption in the FBI leadership, to include the Director, and the numerous unconstitutional acts the agency, at all levels, were committing.

During the Sanchez investigation, Jim was a silent partner in a private security company group, WATCH24, which he trusted and used often in 2010. As a result of their work and fine reputation, WATCH24 had tripled in size in the last 12 years, and Jim is now the President and General Monroe is the Chairman of the Board. Six years ago, Jim had WATCH24 install up-to-date security and surveillance systems in each of our homes which is monitored 24/7. That has given all of us a higher level of safety and comfort.

Since the group was fully aware of the corruption in the Department of Justice and their agencies, we knew that we could not rely on the federal government for any information or aid. Without any apprehension, Jim stated that WATCH24 would be able to help fill that void.

Steve Mason, who retired as the United States Attorney General, was also the US Attorney for the Eastern District Virginia and the prosecutor for the Sanchez investigation. His work with the grand jury during that investigation resulted in a record number of indictments of White House staff members and seven "deep state" associates.

Joe Wells is a retired Central Intelligence Agency analyst and is one of the finest video/audio technicians in this country. His ability is so well known in the industry, he often does contract work throughout the world for WATCH24.

Chief Justice John C. Walters, who has always been a law and order judge, retired from the Supreme Court two years ago. However, he still pays close attention to the cases and the major law enforcement events throughout the country.

Tom Wilson, the Director of the FBI, became the seventh member of our group. The FBI support of our group and WATCH24 agents was outstanding and made an enormous difference. I tell you this because Tom was the last professional Director of the FBI with complete integrity. The next two Directors and the current Director are corrupt, and overtly ignore the Constitution. There are several current investigations of the FBI and a Special Prosecutor has been appointed. What troubles me the most is that the leadership is spreading the corruption to the agent level of the FBI. It is difficult for the FBI to deny this when they give orders to agents that violate their oath of office. And the agents are intelligent enough to know they are violating their oath and no one says a word about it. Are they concerned about losing their jobs or has selling your soul become an acceptable practice in the Bureau? The FBI will never be able to survive for very long without restoring integrity.

After seeing the Antifa riots, destruction of property and lack of prosecution, Judge Walters called Jim and asked, "What are we going to do about all this lack of law and order in America? We desperately need to get our group together ASAP."

And that was exactly what we did.

"Let's start by listing all the actions of the current administration that we believe are destroying our way of life in America and then we will move on and discuss the main characters responsible for each action," suggested General John Monroe.

"I will go first," said Steve Mason. "The number one responsibility for any government in a democracy is public safety which means there must be law and order in the country," stated Steve.

Joe responded at once, "And what do we have now, an administration that wants to defund the police, tie their hands with executive orders and eliminate no-knock warrants. More officers are being killed on the street or are dying from COVID. Antifa rioters are looting businesses and burning down buildings and the police are ordered 'to stand down.' Officers are retiring at a rate never seen before and departments are not hiring or able to attract enough applicants to fill their vacant positions. Police arrests are down substantially, felons are released without bail. Petty larcenies are no longer prosecuted allowing anyone to walk into any store they choose and walk out with shopping carts of stolen goods. There is no law and order left in America."

I had to add my part, "Have you looked at the increases in homicide lately? Major cities across America are seeing an alarming increase in homicides like New York, Philadelphia, and Chicago, the third largest city in the United States, is on pace to have its worst murder rate in 25 years with over 650 homicides in 2021. There is also a rising trend in homicides in smaller cities and overall, America has witnessed a 30 percent increase in homicides in the past few years."

Judge Walters jumped in, "Let us not forget we now have a two-tiered justice system that ignores the crimes of the politicians of one party and has the FBI unconstitutionally raid homes and charge the opposing party with bogus crimes. How does it all end? Aristotle told us in 321 BC when he stated,

Not only life but living with others is possible because of the law. Without law, no man could be assured of the fruits of his labors. Without law, brute force would prevail, the weak would be destroyed by the strong and the strong would destroy themselves in their struggles for ascendancy. Without law, there would be no peace or privacy, no protection of persons or property, public or private; no foreseeable future, no assurance of anything we could count on.

"And that is only one of the problems we are facing," Joe said to end the law and order discussion. "And we have so many others to discuss, let's keep going. Let's be open and honest here. The

President along with his son are corrupt, the Department of Justice is corrupt, a large part of the upper echelons of the FBI is corrupt, the Secret Service is under investigation and all the intelligence agencies have corruption problems. We are trying to save America from becoming a Banana Republic. We may be too late."

"Let's pray that it is not too late," Jim added. "There is no doubt that America is facing an extraordinary challenge that few expected. The quest to bring socialism to America by the radical left has polarized our country tremendously.

However, we cannot fix everything that is wrong with our country. But if we can eliminate the corruption in the White House and the Department of Justice, it will impact the entire federal government forcing compliance with the Constitution and the return of law and order. And there is no doubt in my mind, that the corruption investigation will lead to the President and his son. I trust that will result to an impeachment or his resignation. And then it is up to the new administration to get America back on track, unify our country, and work together for the greater good."

When we all agreed to bring the group back together for this initial meeting, I made a list of events, or crises to be more exact, that I fully believe are tearing apart America and are not only creating anxiety in this country, but throughout the entire free world.

1. Lack of law and order, which we already discussed to a degree. And the first step, I think we will all agree, is to obey the United States Constitution without exception. Most people in America have lost their trust in the federal government, and rightfully so. If we are going to unite as a

nation, we must return credibility to our government. With all the lies and misinformation from the President and others during the COVID pandemic, this is much easier stated than done.

2.   The corruption in the 2020 elections can no longer be denied.

3.   With inflation over 8 percent, most American families are struggling to put food on their tables and gas in their cars. And there is no end in sight. In addition, with the empty shelves in the grocery stores, the shortage of baby formula and ever-increasing prices for medicine, household goods and home utilities, the impact on the quality of life has been a disaster for most families in America. Let there be no doubt, the policies of the President and his administration are fully responsible for the hardships we are experiencing.

4.   The President inherited a country that was energy independent when he assumed office. The far left forced their climate change false views on the President and he caved immediately and shut down the oil pipeline and banned offshore drilling in specified areas. Now we are buying energy from Russia, one of our staunchest enemies. As it now stands, transportation and utility costs will consume over 40 percent of the middle class family budget.

5.   The past administration was committed to border security and provided funds to build another one hundred miles of border wall on our southern border. Shortly after his

inauguration, the President issued executive orders shutting down the construction of the border wall and opened the border to anyone and everyone who wanted to come to America, to include terrorists, members of the Mexican drug cartels and MS-13 gangs, human traffickers, and felons who have been previously deported.

6. The 2015, the President signed a nuclear agreement with Iran which was too weak to hold Iran accountable, and in 2018, the new President dismantled it. The United States said it would rejoin the agreement if Iran complied with the terms of the original deal, and if it addresses other issues related to alleged ballistic missile stockpiles. Iran has now ramped up its nuclear program, returning to approximately 97 percent of its pre-2015 nuclear capabilities.

7. As soon as he took office in 2021, the President opened the borders by Executive Order without congressional approval and in violation of the law. Since that time, approximately two million undocumented immigrants have entered America without any screening or tests for COVID. And more are entering every day. There are lawsuits pending in the courts and talk about impeaching the President for violating the immigration law, but nothing has changed and the border problem is out of control.

Jim stood up with his notebook in hand and began, "Now that we have discussed the 'state of the state' of our beloved country, we need to have a serious discussion on personal and family safety, coordination, and logistics. As you know, we made several fatal mistakes in our operation twelve years ago. Agent Steve Oates was assassinated, and we lost one of the good guys. Chuck and Kim's home was partially destroyed by a bomb placed in Chuck's car to kill him. Thank God, there were no injuries. There was a home invasion at my home which ended up in a gun battle. Unfortunately, my wife was shot and spent weeks in the hospital and physical therapy. Patricia, who will forever be the love of my life, has become quite capable of doing everything from a wheelchair, and she has never complained.

The last assignment was difficult for all of us, and our families suffered as well. Let's not let that happen again. WATCH24 did outstanding work for us on our last mission, but we certainly could have used additional personnel. I assure you, this time we will have all the resources that we need.

The last time we were up against much more than just corrupt politicians. They had teamed up with the Mexican drug cartel and career criminals who would do whatever it takes to support their operation. One would think that this assignment would be easier since our opponents are mostly crooked politicians with a radical social agenda. I refuse to make that assumption. They have an agenda that has been actively planned for years. It is funded by billionaire radicals who further expanded the deep state in Washington that has permeated all federal agencies to include the enforcement agencies, the intelligence agencies and the Justice Department.

Additionally, millions of dollars are being used to influence the local elections of district attorneys, prosecutors and judges to place their radical, liberal candidates in these positions. You can see the results across the country now. Violent felons are not charged or released with little or no bail. Prosecutors will not authorize arrests for larcenies under one thousand dollars. As evidence of the effectiveness of all this, one could look at the large increases in all violent and property crimes, and the decreases in arrests and convictions. The result is that the safety of the American people has been further jeopardized.

With all the time and money invested in this cause, I remind you that their two main goals are still a New World Order and changing America from the leader of the free world to a weak, powerless socialist nation.

Imagine if they suddenly realize that despite all their efforts, our group can fulfill its goal to save America and they begin to see their life-long dream crumbling at their feet. Desperate people commit desperate acts.

We will be resurrecting most of our rules and standards from twelve years ago, and we will have very few, if any, physical meetings with the seven of us. Technology has changed and we are going to take advantage of it. Joe will take the floor now and explain it to us."

"Thank you, Jim." Joe said as he was standing up. "Let me start by stating that anything you do that does not follow your normal routine could be noted by the FBI or CIA and forwarded to a special office in the White House. In fact, paranoia is so rapidly spreading throughout the Oval Office, I would not be shocked if they did not have someone watching a computer screen right now that shows the six of us in the same room. That's OK. I am certain that they know we meet here once a month on the third Wednesday for lunch. That is why we are meeting here today.

We are doing nothing out of the ordinary, so this meeting is not raising any red flags. However, all our future meetings will be by secure computers. And that is how we will work every day in our new operation, *Patriots' Call,* with the mission to save America.

To fully understand how this will operate, your current cell phone will be a 'digital twin' for each of you. You will receive a new cell phone today which has been programmed as a clone to your current cell phone. This phone changes from traceable to non-traceable depending on the situation, which will be controlled by WATCH24. This will allow us to put your digital twin at any location while you are in another location physically. When your digital twin is active doing his job, your new phone will be made untraceable. However, do not be alarmed, WATCH24 will still know the exact location of both you and your twin.

Later this evening around 7:00 p.m., a WATCH24 agent in a UPS uniform and in a UPS truck will ring your doorbell with a package that falsely requires a signature. Invite him in and the two of you will open the package together. Inside will be your cloned cell phone, a secure laptop computer for our Zoom meetings, and a credit card in the name of each member of your family. The credit card can be tracked by WATCH24 personnel and should always be with the person, so we know the location of each member of your family, every minute of every day. All the instructions and procedures are included, with a telephone number to get answers to any questions from you or your family. As the agent leaves, he will take your current cell phone to give to another WATCH24 agent who will control your digital twin and you will meet in the next day or two."

Jim stood up next to Joe and said, "And each one of you and

every member of your immediate family will have an assigned WATCH24 agent who will not interfere, but always be close by should there be a need or threat. In most cases, you will have the same agent that was with you in 2010.

We are all aware that America is extremely vulnerable to cyberattacks to our electric power grid, our financial systems our telephone/internet service, and a host of other systems. The Ukraine-Russia war has significantly raised the threat level for the USA. Putin has become a madman and has already killed 21,000 civilians in Ukraine. He is no better than Hitler. This week he has threatened our President with retaliation for supplying additional weapons to Ukraine. Unfortunately, I would also not rule out an electromagnetic pulse (EMP) attack which would be devastating to America and could lead to World War III.

One last point before we have lunch. WATCH24 now has both a safe house and an adjacent safe lodge which together can comfortably house forty people. It is fully stocked with food and medical supplies and there will be a medical practitioner there 24/7. If there are any attacks on America, sit tight. Pack a suitcase with clothes, medicine and other necessities, and WATCH24 agents will be at your location ASAP to bring you and your immediate family to the safe house. All our utilities (electricity, water, etcetera) are shielded against an EMP attack, and you will have all the comforts of home.

Listen carefully! Our conversation on this operation has ended and we will not discuss it again until our first secure Zoom meeting. Let's eat."

"So much of what is best in us is bound up in our love of family, that it remains the measure of our stability because it measures our sense of loyalty. All other pacts of love or fear derive from it and are modeled upon it."

—Haniel Long

CHAPTER 3

A law enforcement career is always challenging for your family. Shift work, missing family functions because of your schedule, late night emergency calls, and the criticism of police actions, all take a toll on your family. However, the inherent danger is always there. We have all heard the stories of the relief when the door opens and the officer has made it through another shift. But unfortunately, there is the other side of the coin when the doorbell rings and a supervisor is standing there with a chaplain and the spouse cries out, "Oh no. Please tell me he (or she) is OK." Sadly, this scenario has been dramatically increasing over the last several years and it is the tragedy we all hope to avoid. And finally, for any officer or agent, the threat of harm to a member of your family is their worst nightmare.

Twelve years ago. I put my wife, Kim, and my two children, Tom and Marie, through too much of the reality of police work. Our house was bombed. They were assigned personal protection which destroyed any routine they had, and a brief time later, they were removed from their schools and friends to a safe house along with their mother. My job caused their entire world to be turned upside down. Now I am heading home from our group meeting. What am I going to say? "Duty calls, here we go again!" That certainly would not be the best approach.

Admittedly, much has changed for our family in the last twelve years. Both Kim and I have retired and are enjoying a more relaxed lifestyle. We both do volunteer work for our church and other civic organizations. We truly have everything we need in life and it feels good to give back for all the blessings we received.

Our son Tom first met Sharon at the safe house. Sharon was the WATCH24 agent assigned to Marie. To say it was love at first sight for Tom, is probably an understatement. After college, Tom joined the FBI as a new agent, and he and Sharon were married shortly after he completed his training. His first assignment was the Baltimore Field Office which allowed them to rent an apartment halfway between their work locations. Three years later, Tom was transferred to the Chicago Field Office. After months in Chicago, Tom considered resigning from the FBI for several reasons. Neither he nor Sharon liked the long-distance relationship. Secondly, the FBI was not what he expected. In over three years and hundreds of completed Form 301's and 302's, Tom had placed handcuffs on only two people, which is not unusual. Tom had lunch with Jim to ask for advice and Jim told him that the FBI was changing. He thought it was becoming more bureaucratic and political than it should be. Jim offered Tom a position at WATCH24. After talking it over with Sharon, Tom returned to Chicago on Monday and resigned from the FBI. In retrospect, given all the corruption in the FBI over the last several years, Tom made the right choice.

After graduating from the College of William and Mary, our daughter Marie accepted a position as a guidance counselor in a Virginia Beach high school. She met her husband, Jason, through a friend and they started dating. In less than two years they were married, and two years later, their daughter Katherine was born. They have a lovely home in Virginia Beach and since Marie is now five months pregnant, she is a stay-at-home mom and plans to homeschool her children, which gives comfort to both her parents.

So, my group's new operation should not have as much an impact on our children's lives as it did when they were younger. However, they will still be protected by WATCH24 personnel if necessary.

When I arrived home, Kim announced that we were going to have a special seafood dinner this evening and I was told to choose the wine.

I responded, "Sounds good to me. Is there anything else I need to do?"

"No, dinner is at six. Just relax," she said. I then went to my study, checked my email, and gathered my thoughts together for tonight's conversation.

The seafood dinner of shrimp and scallops, salad, a baked potato and wine could not have been any better. The conversation was mostly about Marie's pregnancy and the baby shower Kim was planning. I got up from the table to refill our wine glasses and as I sat back down Kim was silent but staring at me. There was a short silence broken by Kim's question, "So when are you going to tell me what the 'DC Seven' are up to?" That is the name that Kim affectionately named our group. "I know that with everything in our country 'going to hell in a hand basket,' you guys are getting itchy and can't sit still any longer."

That is what I love about my wife. She can read me like a book, she pulls no punches, and when there is something on her mind, she lays it on the table.

I responded, "I spent the last several hours planning on how I was going to start this conversation. I should have known better. Yes, we discussed America's rapid decline today and the corruption in the White House and the federal government. And we did discuss how we could be effective and possibly save our country and way of life. But we vowed that we would do it differently, and not repeat the previous mistakes."

"Chuck, it has to be different. There is no way that I will stay in this house by myself this time. If you aren't going to be here, neither will I," Kim stated emphatically.

"I understand and I feel the same way," I said.

I spent the next hour telling Kim how different it would be this time explaining the Zoom meetings from home and all the safety procedures developed for all of us. When I finished, Kim said, "I feel much better now that you've explain it, but I will never stay in this house at night without you."

I replied, "And I agree," just as the doorbell rang.

I opened the door and there stood Ben from WATCH24, who was one of our assigned agents at the safe house twelve years ago. I invited him in and closed the door. I shook his hand and

Kim hugged him as we expressed how great it was to see him and jokingly, commented on how nice he looked in his UPS shirt. Ben had fifteen minutes to go over the phone, laptop and two credit cards. Otherwise, a UPS truck parked in front of the house for a long time would look strange. As he was leaving, I handed him my cell phone which he immediately put in a lead-lined bag to prevent any signal.

As he left, I turned to Kim and said, "Now there is two of me, the physical Chuck and the digital Chuck."

"There is one last step that Tom is going to oversee," I told Kim. "Tom already has his tracking credit card. He and Sharon are going to Virginia Beach this weekend to give Marie and Jason their credit card and talk to both about safety. They will introduce them to the WATCH24 agent assigned to protect them. With the agent and the surveillance/security system in their home, they are safe."

"There is no worse mistake in public leadership than to hold out false hopes soon to be swept away."
   —Sir Winston Churchill

CHAPTER 4

I must be honest. Having a secure Zoom group meeting from home was a learning experience for me and probably for all of us. But I was pleasantly surprised how much information can be distributed in an hour.

Just like true bureaucrats, the first goal was to set down the guidelines for our group's activity. Jim and Judge Walters drafted the following for our discussion:

- *This operation will be named Patriot's Call, which is our call to all patriots to rally round and help save this great nation.*

- *This group, organization, or whatever you want to think it is does not exist.*

- *Our individual authority for what we are about to do comes from our oath of office "to defend the Constitution of the United States against all enemies, foreign and domestic." Confidentially, this week each of you will be sworn in as a federal agent by the sitting Chief Judge.*

- *No one is above the law and that includes all of us.*
- *There are no politics here. We are seeking the truth—nothing more—nothing less.*
- *There is no intent here to cause the overthrow or destruction of our government. To do so would certainly be against the Smith Act and certainly result in our arrests. We are trying to save America by deciding if and what laws are being violated and presenting all our findings to a grand jury.*
- *When necessary, discreet meetings in public will be between two people only.*
- *Anything that needs to be reported will be documented in your secure laptop and handwritten notes will be destroyed. Remember, time and dates are important.*
- *All evidence will be processed and stored exactly as outlined in the policy and evidence forms on your laptop.*
- *Any purchase pertaining to the investigation will be by cash. Reimbursement forms are on the computer.*
- *Always use your WATCH24 cell phone for sensitive or classified material and all conference calls.*
- *When you are out running errands or going to dinner, etc., assume someone is watching and keep altering your pattern.*
- *You will receive a single secure call to your cell if we must move you and/or your family to a safe house. Your assigned WATCH24 agent, who will be referred to as your shadow, will be at your back door. The agent has the house keys and pass codes for your alarm system should there be a need to enter your home.*
- *The 24/7 emergency number for WATCH24 is programmed*

into your cell. Call if you or any member of your family sees anything unusual or strange, no matter how insignificant you think it may be. Remember, we can immediately check all your surveillance cameras as soon as you call.

Next on our agenda was an update from Jim on the dirty bombs:

"We checked the National Criminal Information Center for all mid-size trucks stolen within fifty miles of the Mexican/Texas Border," Jim began. We have eighty-six vehicles that were reported stolen in the last ten days. Most of them were U-Haul, Ryder, and Amazon. NCIC has placed an "extreme caution- possible dirty bomb" notice on each of these trucks. WATCH24 will update the list daily on your computer and a forensic unit will check for any trace evidence on any truck recovered and report any positive hits.

"Does anyone know where the dirty bombs originated?" asked General Monroe. "It certainly was not Mexico."

"I asked that same question twelve years ago." added Joe. "And the CIA told me they were not sure where they came from. If we did not have trace evidence, I would question if they actually were dirty bombs. Jim, do you think the FBI has any information on this?"

Jim said, "I am not sure they would tell me if they did. The Director is not really a friend of mine."

"It's jealousy. That's because he knows you are sharper than he is. Butter him up and lie to him and tell him he is doing a wonderful job." I sarcastically said.

"You know it is against the law to lie to the FBI," Steve added with a big grin on his face.

Judge Waters jumped into the conversation, "One must

remember the cardinal rule of Washington DC. It is also against the law to lie to Congress, and a sin to question anything they say."

"This has gone far enough and I am offended." Joe stated. "We all know that the CIA is the premier lying agency."

"That is no longer true," I told Joe. "The White House is the real winner here; you can't count all the lies from the President, Vice President and the Press Secretary each and every day."

We all laughed, but it really is a sad connotation that what we just said in jest, is true.

General Monroe put us back on track by saying, "If you look at all the problems our country has faced in the last eighteen months or the problems we are facing today, it all comes back to leadership. Take the evacuation of Afghanistan for example. In all my years in the military, I have never seen a disaster like this one. I could give you dozens of reasons why it failed, and I hold the Chairman of the Joint Chiefs of Staff responsible. There is only way to say it. He would not make a pimple on a good soldier's ass!

Now look at the COVID fiasco, our borders, the inflation we are seeing in our food and gas prices, our increase in crime, the Russian/Ukrainian War, the threat of Communist China, North Korea and Iran, the baby formula shortage, the corruption in our federal government, a weakened military, and a US Constitution that is ignored. What is the common thread here? I will tell you without hesitation. It is the lack of leadership in this White House. If we want to save America, we need to change who sits in the Oval Office. Unfortunately, Congress knows this is true, but their allegiance is to their political party, who has made over fifty percent of them millionaires on a $174,000 annual salary. In comparison, there is only one percent millionaires in the rest of the United States population. If you need a barometer to measure the corruption in Congress, this would be a good one.

I would like to express where I see a solution to our problem. The President is also the Commander-in-Chief of all our armed forces. Currently, there are 2.4 million active and reserve military personnel. There are also 18.8 million veterans in America. I am not sure of the exact percentage, but I would bet that at least eighty percentage of them would cast a vote of "No Confidence" as Commander-in-Chief for the President. That would mean that close to seventeen million Americans with military experience do not think that the President is capable of serving as Commander-in-Chief. Given the volatility the entire world is facing now, his latest poll numbers and the fear of a stunning defeat by the opposing political party, I believe that the President's own party members will ask him to resign so they have a chance to be re-elected. That's why I am working with all the military associations, the American Legion, the Vietnam Veterans of America, the Veterans of Foreign Wars, and other veteran organizations to make sure that everyone knows America is united when it comes to national defense and we desperately need a new Commander-in-Chief."

Jim closed by saying, "Not that this is a problem with this group, but I have always believed you should never lose your sense of humor regardless of the seriousness of the matter in hand. So, posting a thought or story that brings a smile to our faces helps keep us grounded."

Gun Logic

1. Eleven teens die each day because of texting while driving. Maybe it's time to raise the age of Smart Phone ownership to 21.

2. If gun control laws were actually enforced and worked, Chicago would be Mayberry, USA.

3. The Second Amendment makes more women equal than the entire feminist movement.

4. Legal gun owners have three hundred million guns and probably a trillion rounds of ammo. Seriously, folks, if we were the problem, you'd know it.

5. When JFK was killed, nobody blamed the rifle.

6. The NRA or National Rifle Association murders zero people and receives nothing (zero) in government funds. Planned Parenthood aborts 350,000 babies every year and receives $500,000,000 in tax dollars annually.

7. I have no problem with vigorous background checks when it comes to firearms. While we're at it, let's do the same when it comes to immigration, voter ID, and candidates running for office.

8. Folks keep talking about another Civil War. One side knows how to shoot and probably has a trillion rounds. The other side has crying closets and is confused about which bathroom to use. Now tell me, how do you think that would end?

There is a lot of truth here!

"We are not weak if we make a proper use of those means which the God of Nature has placed in our power... the battle, sir, is not to the strong alone it is to the vigilant, the active, the brave."
      —Patrick Henry

CHAPTER 5

Each member of the group received the following text from Jim:

"Our digital twins are going to be remarkably busy next Tuesday. They will be attending a 9:00 a.m. meeting in a small conference room at the Mayflower Hotel on Connecticut Avenue in DC. Given the history we had with the Mayflower, it is only proper that we use this hotel. And as you know, the head of security is a good friend and is always discreet.

Our reason for the meeting is to determine if our group is under any type of surveillance by the current administration. There will be WATCH24 agents watching every door to determine if there is a response by the FBI. I hope they are monitoring our movement and decide to respond. That will give us another valuable tool that will help greatly. Your cells will be placed in the "off" tracking mode during this operation on Tuesday and you are grounded in your house as well. If that is a problem, please let me know. I will update you on Tuesday afternoon."

Early Tuesday morning, the seven WATCH24 "shadow" agents each drove to their assigned group members' home and pulled into the driveway. They then removed the old cell from the lead-lined bag and started the drive to the Mayflower Hotel. Once at the hotel, Joe's shadow had a key to the employee side door that was not covered by a camera and close to the meeting room. They entered the hotel through this door and sat in a chair in the meeting room at exactly 9:00 a.m. They left the room at 9:18 a.m., left the hotel through the same door and drove back to the home where they started. They parked in the driveway, put the cell phone back in the bag, turned the other cell phone tracking to "on," and left the area.

While all this was occurring, another group of WATCH24 agents were in the hotel to determine if there was any response from the FBI. A man and woman (couple) were in the lobby having a cup of coffee and reading the papers. There was another agent sitting in a chair close to the check-in counter on his cell phone who could take pictures if necessary. He also had a fifty-dollar bill which he needed broken down if he needed to be at the counter. There were two agents, a man and a woman who booked rooms for the night and were at opposite sides of the lobby, ready to check out, so they could hear the conversation if any FBI agents arrived and started to ask questions. There were also four WATCH24 agents outside watching to see if there was any response from the FBI, so they could alert the team in the hotel and take photos of the FBI agents and their vehicles.

It wasn't until 2:20 p.m. that Jim let us know if all of this produced anything:

"Bingo! Our seven "shadow" agents and seven "digital" agents did a great job. Three FBI agents in two vehicles arrived at the Mayflower at 9:52 a.m. Evidently, they wanted to finish their coffee first. Their timing didn't indicate they were in a real rush, so I guess their running from their cars to the lobby was for show. They immediately went to the counter and asked if they had seven men using one of their meeting rooms this morning. The hotel employee asked if they had the name of the group or if they knew which room they were using. That must have ticked them off. One of them said, "if we knew that , we would not be talking to you." They then pulled out their FBI credentials and another agent asked, "Will this help your memory?" The hotel employee said, "Not really, but if you tell me the time, I could give you a list that may help you."

"Nine o'clock." said one of them.

"Let me see," the employee said. 'There were four groups meeting at that time. However, I do not know the gender of the participants. The Liberty Insurance group met in Conference Room 201; the New Mother Training Group met in 203; the Merry Gee's met in 205; the Climate Change group met in 207. When we have just a few groups, we separate them in case they get loud."

"Who in the hell are the Merry Gee's?" asked the FBI agent who pulled his credentials.

"Í do not know, but it must be a happy group," was the reply.

The same agent stated, "Jim, it must be the Liberty Group. Can we see that room now?" he asked the employee.

The clerk called the Director of Security and he came to the counter to escort the FBI agents to Room 201. It is our understanding that the FBI asked the leader of the Liberty Insurance group to come out in the hallway where they had an eight-minute conversation and exchanged cards. They then checked all the other rooms and when they opened the door to 205, one of them stated, "Looks like the happy people didn't show up."

As soon as they headed back down to the lobby, one of our agents knocked on the Liberty Insurance group's door and said, "Could we have another one of your business cards?

The man said, "Sure," and handed him a card. We may want to speak to him later.

We have pictures of the three agents and the two vehicles with plate numbers and VIN numbers.

All the WATCH24 involved in the operation are presently in a room to critique the operation and complete the after-action report. I will review it in the next two days and we will discuss it at the next Zoom meeting.

And yes, the "Merry Gee's" is the name for our group and it is more appropriate than you think."

"We live in an age of the sensational, not the sensible."
—Professor/Attorney Johnathan Turley

CHAPTER SIX

Early on Friday morning, Judge Walters emailed the following message to our group on our secure cell phones:

"If any person does not believe that America is now a 'Banana Republic' they need only to understand what took place last night. The January Sixth Committee hearing that aired on ABC last evening, not only proves it, but also certainly validates the actions of this group.

Those who chose to watch it, have witnessed the United States Constitution being shredded, the media denying its civic duty as the fourth leg of democracy, members of Congress lying (which has become the norm in Washington, DC), and political theater. In other words, in full public display to the world, America has exposed all the ingredients required to change a republic democracy to a Banana Republic in a relatively brief period.

Even though the FBI and the Justice Department's extensive investigation did not find any planned insurrection on January 6, the Committee ignored a recent Supreme Court decision and illegally issued a storm of subpoenas. Congress did not like the finding of the FBI/DOJ investigation, so they decided to replace it with their own investigation by a special committee chosen by one party and all rights to the accused were denied. In summary, the Constitution and the Balance of Power were thrown out of the window and the door was opened which allowed the Banana Republic to enter. We have our work cut out for us!"

My first thought was that we are witnessing the birth of long-planned major changes to our country that have been in the works for years and are funded by the world's most radical socialists who want to destroy America. Although there was a concern by many that the January Sixth demonstration could be much larger than anticipated, the requests for additional law enforcement resources and mobilizing the National Guard were denied by the Speaker of the House. Now we know why.

I called Jim and he answered the phone immediately.

"I already read it," he said, "and it is sobering even though we knew where this was heading. I would say that we need to step up our game and timetable. Think about it and we will all discuss it at the Zoom meeting on Tuesday afternoon. I am on my way out the door to take Patricia to her doctor's appointment."

"I hope all goes well," I said as he hit the end button.

"The difference between genius and stupidity is that genius has its limits"
—Albert Einstein

CHAPTER 7

I told Kim I expected that our Zoom meeting today would go into overtime, so she should pick a place for dinner this evening and we would leave as soon as the meeting was over.

She did not hesitate at all and said, "Sure, I have two in mind." Great, I thought. Now I do not have to be concerned about long winded discussions.

The meeting began right on time at 2:00 p.m. After the greetings and the required senior health checks which come with age and were all positive, Jim jumped right in.

"As I told you last week, the digital meeting went very well and now we know for sure that we are under an unlawful surveillance by the FBI and I have not ruled out that other federal agencies may be involved as well. The more information we have, the better we can plan.

Given our experience, we all know the value of paranoia in both war and criminal cases. We now know that the FBI is paranoid which is not unusual in an organization that does not follow the law or the rules or established standards. The more paranoid they become, the higher the chance they will make a mistake. However, there is a downside to this also. Along with the increase in fear and paranoia, comes desperation. Our goal is to increase it enough for them to make a mistake but not cross the line where desperation creates danger for us or the FBI. Think about it and we will discuss this later."

"Tom," Jim said, "with all your years in the FBI, please give us your perspective on all of this."

Tom started by saying, "Sorry I missed the first meeting, but I am up to date. Let me start by saying that the FBI of today is certainly not the same FBI when Jim and I were there. I would have to say that it is no longer an investigative agency that made us proud to be a part of. We did not do everything perfect, but as I learned throughout my career, there are other agencies in the state and local government that are just as competent as the FBI and sometimes better. Once you develop that mindset, you care more about making the case rather than being in charge and that improves your relationship with the police departments you work with and allows for true lifetime friendships.

I remember early in my career hearing a cranky older detective referring to the FBI as F_ _ _ ing Bumbling Idiots. That ticked me off. I soon realized he always joked about the FBI and I learned a lot from that detective because he was a hell of a cop. I look at the FBI now and I read about all the corruption in the upper ranks and the Constitution violations by the street agents and I think that detective's description of the FBI would be accurate today.

I am certain that if I were in the FBI now, I would quit before I sold my soul. My heart goes out to all the retired agents that so faithfully were true to their oath of office. They are the real FBI.

I did get information that one of the supervisors in the FBI Washington Field Office did submit a request for use of one of the newer FBI surveillance vehicles. I am going to assume that was a result of the meeting at the Mayflower and I will bet we will find it parked somewhere near the hotel next week.

Joe, would you see if you can find out how that van is equipped and let us know what changes we need to make in our operations. I would suggest that we change our next digital/shadow meeting at the Mayflower to a Sunday morning. As you know, it is almost impossible to find an FBI agent working on Sunday. And by the time the duty agent responds, the digital agents will be back in their bags and all of us will be home eating Sunday dinner."

"Judge, is there anything you want to add on the January 6th Committee or anything we need to know from a military perspective."

"I have several items to discuss," stated Judge Walters.

"The January Sixth Commission television did not get the viewers they expected; the block-buster information they promised never surfaced; there was more misinformation than factual; and of the roughly 570 people arrested, most were charged with minor misdemeanors and only 40 were charged with conspiracy.

Additionally, a poll taken by the Capitol Police officers prior to January 6th, revealed a 90 percent 'No Confidence' vote in the hierarchy of the Department. Most of law enforcement and the public believe that the fatal shooting of an unarmed women veteran by a Capital Police Lieutenant was not a 'good shoot' and a cover-up. And most likely because of all these missteps, polls show that the American people have moved beyond the January Sixth demonstration and are more concerned about the high crime rates, increased gas prices and inflation, food, baby formula and dog food shortages, and illegal immigration.

The second event that needs discussion is the death threat against the Supremes Court judges due to the illegal leak by someone inside the Court. My understanding is that the leak investigation is moving forward but no arrests have been made.

What troubles me even more is the cavalier response from the liberal politicians in Congress who I believe are delighted that the demonstrations at the judges' homes have grown and this somehow helps their cause. Recently we had an arrest made on an overt threat to assassinate one of the Supreme Court judges and another Wisconsin court judge shot to death. The murder of those who enforce society's rules on law and order, whether a law enforcement officer or a judge, for having done their job, is a pure and evil act and is a threat to our democracy. There is no safety in a society without a functioning legal system. We can no longer tolerate this low or no bail policies of these liberal prosecutors."

"Thanks, John," Jim said. "Your turn, General."

"Recruitment is at an all-time low for the military," started the General. "All the idiotic rules on the COVID vaccinations and mandated rules and training for the Critical Race Theory BS have been devastating to the military. We are far from full strength and our readiness factor is dismal. If we continue down this path, we will become a third world country.

'Russia has stepped up the bombing in Ukraine resulting in large increases in civilian deaths," started the General. "There is no support for Russia's aggression throughout the free world. And although Putin continues to deny it, he is losing the support of his own people. It is clear to the entire world that Putin is committing vast genocide, second only to Hitler. His numerous war crimes are far beyond anything we have seen in over 75 years. Perhaps if our President wasn't so weak and showed some leadership skills, the NATO countries and others may have united to end this slaughter. Unfortunately, I do not see any changes under this administration.

I expect that China will attack Taiwan before the November elections, knowing that they have been able to compromise the President and his son to the point that the United States will not take any action against China.

The International Atomic Energy Agency cameras and monitoring equipment that was installed in Iran under the 2015 nuclear deal, are currently being removed by Iran. This action will most likely destroy any chance for a future nuclear deal. My hope is that Israel still has the backbone to take care of the problem. But without the support of a strong military from America, I could not criticize them if they remained idle.

When you look at the entire world picture, a weak, incapable United States President leads to a leadership void throughout the free world which does nothing but embolden our enemies. In all honesty, I cannot rule out a nuclear attack someplace in the world which will most likely lead to World War III. The clock is ticking and I do not know how much time is remaining. And yes, we need to speed up our timetable."

Jim added, "General, we all pray that this day never comes. Sadly, I only see two scenarios that will save us – a rapid change from our current administration or the rapture. At my age, I would accept which ever arrives first. Steve, what is on your mind?"

"Since much of what I heard this afternoon is troubling, I am going to start on a high note," Steve said. "The George Soros backed prosecutor in San Francisco received a "No Confidence" vote and will be out of office very soon. To get a vote like this in liberal California tells me that the tide is turning and the November mid-term elections could be the start to better days.

Now the not so good news. Both violent and property crimes are up in every part of the country. Homicides, to include police officers, are higher. Shootings are out of control in most large metropolitan areas from coast to coast. And the fear of crime factor for families increases each month. Arrests are down. Prosecutions and convictions are lower. More felons are released with little or no bail. The jail population is decreasing. The fact that there are few or no arrests for larceny under $1,000 are destroying our local businesses, which eliminates the tax base. Police resources are declining. The per capita police/citizen ratio declines daily. In some areas, the high price of gas is limiting police responses to violent crimes only and it is difficult for departments to find the funds to replace aging equipment. However, to no one's surprise, all of this has led to a continuous increase in the sale of firearms to the law-abiding citizens who want to protect their families when the police are not available. And in contrast to the beliefs of many of our federally elected officials who all have free protection paid by the taxpayer, the increase in armed citizens is a good thing. Unfortunately, with every shooting, our government lays the responsibility on the armed law-abiding citizens rather than the criminal. This a criminal justice system that has been turned upside down. And I fully agree with the group. If we do not correct these problems quickly, the America that we have grown to love, is doomed.

Jim thanked Steve and stated, "Joe has several items he needs to discuss with us."

Joe opened with, "After listening to everything our country is dealing with, I truly wish I had the technology to fix it all. But we all know that technology does not exist. But I am here to tell you, there is more technology coming out every day than ever before in our history. That is the good news. Unfortunately, I also have shocking news. Let me ask you a few rhetorical questions. Do you trust Russia? Do you trust China who floods the United States market with electronics, furniture, food, household items, computers, clothes, shoes, tools, medical equipment, cell phones, personal hygiene products, medicine and much more? Did China attempt to kill as many Americans as possible with release of the COVID virus? Do you trust the big tech companies? Do you trust the World Health Organization? Do you trust your cell carrier? How many of your emails do you think are absolutely true. Do you trust all the ads you read? I can go on and on. But let me ask you one last question. Do you trust your federal government? I am certain that all of us would answer "no" to most of these questions. Would it surprise you if I told you that the younger generation and your grandchildren would answer "Yes" to these questions?

I am mostly a positive person. But people have no idea how sinister people, governments and corporations can be. If China really decided to destroy America, how long would it take for us to learn that they were slowly killing us with the medicine they send to America every day? Think about it.

Let's be candid here. The federal government monitors almost everything we do and they are extremely interested in every word each of you mutter. And they have a team that works on this every day. I have new equipment that I will be installing in your house which will alert you and WATCH24 every time there is any surveillance equipment in range of your home. You will be notified by a tone and text message on your secure cell. You do not have to ever worry about anything you buy or bring into your home. If there is a problem, we will know in less than thirty seconds.

I will be making my rounds next week to upgrade your and your family's security system and install new innovative technology. I will call you on you cell to find a suitable time for both of us. Thank you."

Jim then said, "Chuck, how about giving us your thoughts and closing comments."

"Thanks Jim." I said." I do not know about the rest of you, but after hearing how many serious problems this country is facing with a President who is corrupt, cognitively challenged, and inept, my sense of urgency is at its highest level and I will not sleep very well tonight. I, for one, am not sure who is running our federal government. But I will get that answer by the next meeting."

Jim concluded, "As a profoundly serious ending note, I must say that we are being defeated from within our own borders by the elected officials who are sworn to preserve, protect, and defend the Constitution of the United States. They have determined that the enemy is the American people who are not liberal socialists, who bow to their every command. They are guilty of treason, should be impeached, removed from office, stripped of their pensions and jailed. That may be what is necessary to save America. Stay safe out there. The world is upside down."

"The First Amendment provides a safeguard for all Americans and remains the most effective protection of religious liberty, free speech and peaceful assembly in the world."
—Unknown

CHAPTER 8

I was correct yesterday when I told the group that I wouldn't be able to sleep tonight. I did not. It was sometime after 4:30 a.m. that I fell asleep. I was shocked when I looked at the clock and saw it was 9:00 a.m. I immediately dressed and headed toward the kitchen. Kim greeted me with a smile, "Good morning, Sleeping Beauty. I guess you had a tough night last night."

I replied, "I did."

Kim continued, "Did you remember that Tom and Sharon are coming to dinner tonight and they will be here at five, so you can have time together and Sharon and I can get caught up. Dinner is at six."

I said, "I did remember, thanks."

Tom and Sharon are highly organized and always punctual, so I was not surprised that the doorbell rang at exactly 5:00 p.m. If

Marie and Jason were coming to dinner, the doorbell would ring between 5:15 and 5:30 p.m. and Kim would have planned dinner for 6:30 p.m.

After the greetings with hugs and kisses in the foyer, Tom and I grabbed a beer and headed for the den and the ladies poured two glasses of wine and sat at the kitchen table.

As soon as we sat down, Tom said, "Dad, you probably know that I have been assigned as your 'shadow' and I am in control of your digital twin."

I replied. "Of course, I do. And I wouldn't have it any other way. And Sharon has been assigned to the team that will watch over Marie's family. Are you and Sharon OK with all of this?"

"Are you kidding me Dad," Tom said with enthusiasm. "Every time Sharon and I read the paper or watch the news, we are troubled by the decline in our country and were hoping your group would get active again. This is a dream come true for us and for most of America. And to be honest, it always bothered me that I sat on the sidelines during the Sanchez investigation and now both Sharon and I have the greatest feeling being a part of this operation."

"Do you have any apprehensions or regrets?" I asked Tom.

"None whatsoever," he answered quickly. In fact, as I look back at the last twelve years of my life, I made two of my best decisions that I will never regret. First, was asking Sharon to marry me and secondly was resigning from the Bureau. I would never allow myself to be a part of an organization that I have no respect for."

"I have one more family issue we need to discuss," I told Tom. "How do you think Marie and Jason will manage all of this?"

"I know for sure that Marie will feel much better knowing Sharon is assigned to the team that will take care of them,"

Tom stated. "Marie's concerns center around family. She will be concerned about all of us and right now she wants to make sure she has a healthy baby. Sharon and I will most likely be spending more time with them and I am sure there will be nights that Sharon stays in their guest room. We both know that Marie is a strong person and she and Jason will be fine."

"And her mother is already planning on stocking up on baby formula, so that problem is resolved," I told him and we both had a little laugh.

After Tom and Sharon left at 8:00 p.m., we followed our parent protocol and sat down, discussed each of our conversations. I knew instantly that she was much more comfortable with our new operation. And at the end of the evening, we commented how lucky we were to have such a wonderful family. And then we said a prayer for all of us.

"A lie doesn't become truth, wrong doesn't become right, and evil doesn't become good, just because it's accepted by the majority."
—Rick Warren

CHAPTER 9

We had several days when there were no emails or text messages from the group. We all needed time to sort out all the current information and plan our next move. I rather enjoyed the break, but at the same time, I know we had to speed up our schedule to save our rapidly denigrating country.

Our rest and relaxation ended with Jim's text message on Monday:

"Here is my latest update. If anyone else has an update, please text everyone.

As we expected, the FBI surveillance van is parked across from the Mayflower Hotel. It is a dark gray SUV with tinted windows and climate change and green peace stickers on the rear window. They are a day early and we are going to let them sit there for five or six days. If they leave, we may make our move early Sunday morning, so you may have to change to another time for church. I will let you know by 4:00 p.m. on Saturday.

We are going to step it up a notch for the next meeting and add a woman to your digital twins. More on this later.

Interestingly, a group of five Navy Seals who are running for office, stood on the steps of the United States Capitol and stated the following:

'We never thought we would have to serve at home, but the United States is in danger of becoming a socialist dictatorship thanks to members of Congress who hate our freedoms, using any excuse and any mandate to take them away.'

This is a great message from true patriotic heroes that will certainly help all of us.

It has been reported that North Korean leader Kim Jong Un has doubled down on his arms buildup and may soon begin nuclear test explosions. In addition, China has stated they would go to war "no matter what the cost' with the United States if we make any effort to maintain Taiwan's independence.

Ukrainian and British officials warned this week that Russian forces are using more deadly weapons, most likely 6.1-ton anti-ship missiles to make headway in eastern Ukraine, causing mass casualties of up to one thousand citizens a day.

This is what happens when we have a weak, inept President and Cabinet. Russia, China, Iran and North Korea are taking full advantage of our weakness.

And finally, the FBI continues to act in their chosen role as a political law enforcement agency for the liberal left, making unwarranted physical misdemeanor arrests and using leg irons which have only been used in the past for the most violent felons and for those who are a flight risk. Welcome to our two-tiered justice, Banana Republic. Pray for the world."

Jim gave us a subliminal message in his last four words. When we decided to start this operation, our goal was to save America. While that may be true, if we are successful, we may actually save the world. That is a lot of weight to put on the shoulders of seven men.

Jim is true to his word. At 3:45 p.m. on Saturday, He sent the following text:

"We are a 'go' for a digital meeting tomorrow morning. All of you are grounded from 6:00 a.m. to 8:00 a.m.
There will be a short Zoom meeting at 1:00 p.m., Monday afternoon."

"If science cannot be questioned, and debate is denied, it isn't science anymore. It's propaganda."
—Unknown

CHAPTER TEN

Jim sent out a short text message at 8:15, Sunday morning:

"This morning's digital meeting went very well with a few twists to it. We still have covert agents on the scene to document any FBI response. We will have a full briefing tomorrow.

Enjoy your day."

That was good news. I am not exactly sure what Jim means by "a few twists," but tomorrow's Zoom meeting should prove to be most interesting.

With everyone online for the Monday morning Zoom meeting, I could tell that Jim was anxious to get started and seeing the smile on his face, I knew it was good news.

Jim asked, "Does everyone remember Carol from WATCH24, who was with Kim during the explosion at their home twelve years ago? She is still with us and highly active in this investigation. She is the eighth digital person who attended yesterday' s meeting at the Mayflower. Let me explain.

Last week I asked Carol to purchase a "throw away" cell phone from a 7-11 store in northern Virginia. Joe modified the phone so he could control the signal emitting from the phone when necessary. We also made sure that the 7-11 store had working cameras. Carol, in a disguise that we designed and wearing a KN95 white face mask, entered the 7-11 and paid cash for the cell phone. The transaction took less than five minutes, which should give the FBI some good video. Carol left the store and walked several blocks to a bus stop. As planned, in less than a minute she was on the bus. Eight minutes later, she got off the bus where we knew there were no active surveillance cameras, went around the corner and was picked up by another WATCH24 agent.

We placed eleven strategic calls from the phone and staged twelve incoming calls to the phone. This morning Carol and her digital twin attended the meeting at the Mayflower. Unfortunately, but as planned, Carol dropped a small silver mirror/compact case engraved with the initials "MG." There are numerous fingerprints on the case, but none of them belong to Carol. The WATCH24 report confirms that the FBI did respond to the Mayflower, but not until 9:35 a.m. However, the FBI agents did search the room and now have the silver case.

But what do the initials 'MG' stand for? It must be for the "Merry Gees,' the group that reserves the meeting rooms. Or could it be Mary Gray, who last month resigned from her position on the Vice President's staff. Or it could be for Megan Gunter, a law clerk in the Supreme Court, who just hired an attorney when she was asked to produce her cell phone records in relation to the *Roe vs. Wade* leak investigation. I am not sure. What a coincidence."

The laughter that followed interrupted Jim's presentation. When it died down, Jim continued, "Paranoia is a powerful tool!"

"On a much more serious note, our country continues its rapid downhill spiral. We are at a forty-year record high inflation rate which is approaching fifteen percent. The violent crime rate is out of control and the police are retiring in record numbers. Everything this President touches is a disaster. This administration's relentless assault on our God-given rights continues. This week, the Supreme Court will release their *Roe vs. Wade* decision and we expect riots across America. What should keep us awake at night, is that this is entirely intentional by the left social politicians who want to destroy America. We are running out of time.

I know we talk about this all the time, but this is treason pure and simple. Steve, I want you to spend time with the treason statutes, and match all the events, conduct, speeches threats and anything you may want to add that is a covert act by the social left and draw up an outline for indicting these people.

Judge, confidently touch base with the Chief Judge of the Supreme Court and figure someway for you and Steve to receive the authority to sit a grand jury. Remind the Chief Judge that we have precedence since we did it twelve years ago.

Our Zoom meetings need to be more frequent, and for now will be every Monday and Thursday at 10:00 a.m. in the morning. The next one will be Thursday morning. Remember, anyone of you can call for an emergency meeting any time, day or night.

Do any of you have any information that cannot wait until Thursday? Hearing no response, let me leave you with this from

Thomas Paine:

> *'I love the man that can smile in trouble, that can gather strength from distress, and grow brave by reflection. Tis the business of little minds to shrink; but he whose heart is firm, and whose conscience approves his conduct, will pursue his principles unto death.'*

What a sobering thought. Stay safe and we will meet again on Thursday."

We are all aware that Jim is pushing the needle, and that is exactly what we should be doing. The social left has thousands of people and millions of dollars pushing their agenda. But I take comfort because I have faith, knowing that it is in God's hands.

In a little more than an hour after the meeting, I received a call from Jim.

"Hey, Jim," I answered. "What's up?"

"Things are going faster than I expected," Jim started. I just got a phone call from Assistant Special Agent-in-Charge Nick Brown, who is a supervisor in the Washington Field Office of the FBI. He asked me to come to his office for a chat. I first asked him what the chat was about. His response was, 'I will tell you when you get here.' I told him that does not work for me.

His answer did surprise me. He stated, 'You know Jim, we really do need to talk and I think you would find it to be an interesting conversation.'

What do you think?"

I said, "I think you did the right thing. You know, years ago we would have gone to his office, walked in and said, 'What's up?' Watching the actions of the FBI over recent years, most of America would tell them to go to Hell. As you wished, their paranoia factor is rising. I think you should document it the best you can and call Steve and let him know. Then I would sit on it and see what happens."

"Good advice," Jim said. "That is what I will do. And by the way, I recorded the conversation." And he ended the call.

Jim did not have to tell me he recorded the conversation. There was never a doubt in my mind.

"What the herd hates most is the one who thinks differently. It is not so much the opinion itself, as the audacity of wanting to think for themselves. Something they do not know how to do."
—Schodenhauer

CHAPTER 11

The Thursday Zoom meeting began with Jim telling the complete group about the call from the Washington Field Office. Everyone agreed with Jim's decision.

Jim suggested that it would be best if Tom Wilson serves as the group liaison with the FBI if there is a need since he retired as Director.

Tom added, "I really do not see a scenario that would require me to talk to anyone in the FBI until they get their act together, but I will take care of it.

There was a second discussion on the January 6th Committee hearings. Again, there was consensus that the Committee and the media were "overselling" what they uncovered and with all the witnesses reading off a teleprompter, the credibility of the entire report is in jeopardy. The last point centered on how the entire fiasco is further splitting the American people. This is a goal where the socialist left may gain ground, but the mid-term elections will provide the eventual answer.

The last topic of the day was an update on the dirty bombs which started with Joe asking, "Has anyone heard anything on the search for the dirty bombs? First, I have checked with a contact in the CIA and the file has not been updated in years. Secondly, I know there was allegedly trace evidence, but what that means is unclear. Does that confirm the quality of the uranium is high enough to be effective? Does that confirm that the bombs truly exist in a condition that they could be deployed? Third, does the Mexican cartel have the expertise to explode a nuclear bomb without killing themselves and everyone else in a 500-to-1000-mile radius? And fourth, money is more important to the cartel than revenge. Could they have the bombs up for sale to Iran or North Korea, countries that currently do not have nuclear bomb capabilities? I would think not or the CIA would certainly get wind of it if they still operated the same as they did when I was there. And my final question, is all this bullshit and there are no bombs and the cartel is holding out for ransom payments from our inept, weak government?"

After a lengthy discussion, we realized our government appears to not have the answers to these questions. Unbelievable, given the money and resources we have provided for national intelligence!

Jim asked for Joe and Tom to see if they could get answers and report back to the group.

Another Zoom meeting that leaves all of us with our head spinning and more questions than answers. If the public knew how screwed up and corrupt our federal government has become, they would also be awake at night.

On Friday morning at 12:22 a.m., my phone rang. I hate calls at this time in the morning because they are seldom good news. I grabbed my phone and went into the den so Kim could sleep.

I answered the phone and Jim said, "Chuck, I have Joe on the line and he has a story to tell us. Go ahead Joe."

"Good morning, Chuck, sorry to bother you so early, but I just caught a guy breaking into my SUV. It wasn't until I stuck a gun in his face that I learned he was an FBI agent named Mark Lawton. Right now, he is sitting in a lawn chair behind my SUV handcuffed to my trailer hitch. You think he would be smarter than that to break into a vehicle belonging to a retired CIA techy. He had to know that I would have surveillance cameras everywhere. In any case, I have his gun, wallet, and credentials locked in the front seat of my SUV. His car is down the road and I have not checked it yet. Not a bad kid. His supervisor told the entire Field Office, that any agent who brings him useful info on our group would get two extra days of vacation. Mark and his wife have a baby at home and he thought it would be easy since he is a trained locksmith. So instead of calling the Sheriff, I thought I would call Jim first."

Jim asked, "Joe, are you okay watching him for about thirty minutes until I can get Tom and Steve out to your house?"

Joe replied, "No problem. He isn't going anywhere. I will just sit next to him in the driveway and give him an ethics lecture."

"Good work, Joe," I said as Joe ended his call leaving Jim and me still connected.

I could not help myself, and blurted, "Paranoia is a valuable tool."

"Yes, it is," Jim stated. "And we are about to reap a massive collection from it."

As expected, my phone rang again at 3:05 a.m. "Yes, Jim," I said.

Jim got right to the point, "Chuck, Steve has a question for us. Go ahead Steve."

Steve began, "Good morning and I mean it. This is a good morning. Given the hour, I will be brief, but we need to have a Zoom meeting this afternoon.

Agent Mark Lawton was a bit overzealous and has overstepped his bounds, but he was candid with us and told us that the Washington Field Office is getting its direction from the White House and the Attorney General with the concurrence of the Director. However, some of the FBI supervisors and most of the agents are upset by the orders they are receiving, and according to Mark, he and many others have decided to document everything and they are awaiting and hoping for 'the day of reckoning.' Joe, Tom and I all think we should give it to them.

We propose releasing Mark and allow him to go home like nothing ever happened. He cannot mention any of this to anyone, including his wife and he is to call his supervisor in the morning and tell him he is sick and needs to stay home today. That will enable us to talk with him in the morning and he will give us his notes and a list of FBI personnel who also have documentation. We need to develop a plan that will protect the FBI whistle blowers and at the same time move quickly. I can give you more information at our meeting. What do you think?"

Jim and I both agreed with the plan so Jim told Steve to go ahead with it and a Zoom meeting would be scheduled for 1:00 p.m.

I went back to bed thinking about how everything seems to be falling into place and instantly I knew how it all came to be. It was not "as luck would have it," but it is "as God would have it." I said a prayer of thanks and praise and fell asleep.

At breakfast, I simply mentioned to Kim that the group was going to move it up a notch or two. Her response did not surprise me. "If you want to save America, you had better be thinking of moving it up ten or twenty notches!

I laughed and said, "I will be sure to relay your suggestion to Jim."

"Make sure you do!" she said seriously. And with a sense of humor, she added with a smile, "And tell Jim to not let them blow up our house again."

Not that the group was anxious, but everyone was logged in fifteen minutes early, so Jim started the meeting.

"Much has taken place within the last twelve hours or so, which may create a different path for us," Jim stated. "And let me say this before I turn it over to Joe, Steve and Tom to bring you up to date. If we are going to save America, the first and most important thing is to restore law and order. Without it, we have nothing. Okay Joe, you are up first."

Joe told his story, pretty much the same as he told it early this morning. In the end, he added, "You can humble a person quite rapidly when you stick a gun in his face and then handcuff him to your trailer hitch. And after he realizes he is lucky to be alive, he quickly understands his life has been turned upside down. And then Mark figures it out that I am not the enemy, but the only one that can save him. Like any decent man, he looks at his heart and soul and bares the truth. And where we are today in this goal to save America, is because FBI Agent Mark Lawton is a good man. And as he was leaving to go home, he turned to the three of us and said, 'Thank you and I promise you that you will not regret this."

Tom Wilson spoke next, "And I need to add a comment on what Joe just said. The other factor that leads us to this path today, is Joe's humanity and outstanding interrogation skills.

After much thought, I called Jim earlier today and told him that I know George Peters who is the FBI Assistant Director who oversees the entire FBI Washington Field Office. When I was the Director, I promoted him to Assistant Special Agent-in-Charge and three years later to Special Agent-in-Charge. I have always thought he was a stand-up guy. I thought about calling him to see if I could get a read on him and see what he says. Jim told me he trusted my judgment and if I thought it would help, to give him a call.

When I did call him and told him who I was, he paused for a few seconds and closed his door. I asked him how he was. His response was, 'I have been better.' I told him that I understood what he was going through and we can make it better. After a short pause, I asked him, 'Are you with me or are you against me?' He replied with enthusiasm, 'Sir, I am with you and I have been waiting for a call like this for a long time. The FBI today is not the FBI you retired from. How can I help you.?'

We talked for a few more minutes and he told me he had covertly documented every misdeed with dates, times, and names. We plan to meet this evening and he will have a package for me. I will tell him about Agent Mark Lawton and let him know that as far as we are concerned, it never happened. And tomorrow, I expect to spend the day reading and tagging evidence.

The group broke into an applause.

Jim stated, "All of you did a fantastic job. Thank you!

However, we know the road gets rough from here. Step back for a moment and look what lies ahead. We will be indicting a substantial number of people who are career FBI employees, Department of Justice employees, and possibly people tied to the White House. Today, all these people believe they are untouchable and are 'on top of the world.' They will be arrested, hopefully convicted, sent to prison, lose their federal pension, and embarrass themselves and their families. Their entire world will come crashing down and they will become desperate but will have few or no places to turn. The history in similar cases tells us that some will consider suicide, and others, unfortunately, may retaliate. We must take every precaution to protect the grand jury, to protect our witnesses and their families, to protect our families and the WATCH24 staff.

My advice to all of you is to enjoy the weekend with your family and get some rest. We are just too old to pull an all-nighter."

His short pause resulted in laughter and comments from everyone.

Jim continued, "There will be a Zoom meeting at 10:00 a.m. Monday morning. Roll up your sleeves, bring any updates or information you have, and let's draw up a plan that will really get this operation moving."

"A dog had his chain reduced one link at a time, every few days, until his chain was so short, he could barely move. He never resisted because he was conditioned to the loss of his freedom slowly, over time. It's happening to Americans."

—Unknown

CHAPTER 12

To begin today's meeting, Jim asked me to give the group an update on the events that impact our country.

"Some of you may have heard some of this," I started. "So, jump in if you have anything to add."

"With the Russia/Ukraine conflict now in its fourth month, Russia is pounding the Donbas region with relentless air raids and artillery daily. Ukraine is losing between 100 and 200 soldiers every day. The world has been slow in providing Ukraine military with the needed offensive weapons and this could prove to be decisive. Not good for a world suffering from the self-inflicted wounds of pandemic policy, especially as the cost of continuing war is destruction, poverty, hunger, and bloodshed. Please keep the Ukrainian people in your prayers.

Recent polls show Americans are 'clearly worried about crime.' Gallup finds that 72 percent of Americans are dissatisfied with the nation's policies to reduce or control crime. Crime looks like it will be one of the top issues for voters this November which will not help the current Administration.

Voters have noticed that cities where shootings occur almost daily also have some of the strictest gun laws, according to *The Wall Street Journal.* Low-income minorities have felt the brunt of liberal policy makers who 'treat criminals like victims and police officers like criminals.'

Steve added, "And the ever-increasing homicide of law enforcement officers continues with three this weekend. Despite what anti-Police activists would have us think, the vast majority of Law Enforcement Officers would give their lives to save others. And we all know, no one hates a bad cop more than good cops."

I continued, "The President has spent trillions trying to 'transform' the country, and now everyone, especially the nation's poorest, is paying the price. Inflation rose to 8.6 percent in May, its highest level in more than 40 years. Again, I pray the voters will remember this in November.

The massive caravan of undocumented immigrants headed for our already overwhelmed southern border is proving to be the best friend the drug cartels ever had, as deadly poisons like fentanyl pour across our border and kill record numbers of Americans.

The Vice President is an unpopular liability for her party and the single best argument they have for trying to keep the President despite his low ratings. My best bet is that the Vice President will be removed from office after the November elections no matter which political party controls the House and the Senate.

And I will close with good news. With the uproar after the *Roe vs. Wade* decision, the House passed a bill extending additional government-funded security to the Supreme Court justices and their families on Wednesday and sent the legislation to the President for final approval."

Jim then asked, "Judge, do you or Steve have an update on the grand jury?"

"I do," Judge Walters replied. "After I conveyed our request to the Chief Judge, he said, 'If there was ever any better time for a special grand jury in all our history, including the Sanchez case, it is now. My only hope is that you are not too late, and my main concern is that you do everything in your power to protect the secrecy of the grand jury.'"

I replied to the Judge that we are already working on the plan and he would have a copy next week.

"Our grand jury protection plan is a bit unusual. We will be using a tour bus from one of the larger tour companies which will be in the large parking lot they always use. The bus driver and the tour guide will be WATCH 24 agents. The 'tourists,' also known as jurists, will be dropped off by a member of the family, which will be a WATCH24 agent and picked up at the end of the day and returned to their home. The judge has approved two extra alternate jurors who are also WATCH24 agents (one male and one female) who will always be there for protection.

Additionally, every witness will have a WATCH24 agent that will serve as their bodyguard. The grand jury will always have a minimum of six agents present.

Steve has again asked Antonio Lopez to collaborate with him with the grand jury and the trials. As you remember, Tony spent years as a prosecutor before he was an FBI attorney and worked with Steve on the Sanchez case. When Steve was the United States Attorney General, he brought in Tony as his number two who retired in 2019."

Jim added, "All the WATCH24 agents assigned to personal protection are retired from the Marshall's Service or have received training in personal protection. They have the best equipment and radio system available, so our jurors and witnesses are well cared for."

Joe was next. He started by asking Tom, "How is my friend Mark doing?" Tom responded, "He is doing good and has recovered from the trauma of having a gun stuck in his face."

Everyone laughed and Joe continued, "I will be placing covert cameras in the bus so we can keep our eyes on it twenty- four hours a day. We have a designated garage to store our bus and cameras on the perimeter. Should we identify anyone who is a threat to our operation, we will tag their vehicles, put surveillance on their residence and make a covert attempt to tag them as well. And one last point, last month we completed a complete upgrade on the safe house and lodge just in case we need to use them."

Jim closed the meeting with a huge smile and stated "I just wanted to remind all you aging seniors. We will always have at least two meetings a week—Monday and Thursday. Anyone of you can call for a meeting, when necessary, just send me a text."

As the meeting closed, I felt that we were making progress, but I had this sick feeling that we were missing something, and I could not put my finger on it. I will feel much better when Tom tells all of us that the evidence he received from Agent Lawton and Assistant Director Peters, is credible.

"What we have done for ourselves alone dies with us; what we have done for others and the world remains and is immortal."
—Albert Pike

CHAPTER 13

AT 6:45 a.m. on Wednesday morning, I was reading the paper and enjoying my second cup of coffee when my phone started vibrating to let me know I had a text message. I picked it up and saw it was a group text from Jim. The message was not exactly what I expected:

"Joe has asked for an emergency Zoom meeting at 8:00 a.m. this morning. Text me and let me know if you are available."

I immediately texted Jim and told him that I was available. I had no idea why Joe wanted a meeting, but I was glad the wait would not be long.

Everyone was available and the meeting began on time with Jim asking Joe to go ahead.

Joe said, "I am sorry to interrupt your morning, but I have essential information to share with you. To put you at ease, this is not at the 'red' level, but it is just below it.

Yesterday at exactly 10:12 p.m., our surveillance camera showed a 2015 dark blue Jeep Cherokee with New York plate AEW- 412 going west slowly past Jim's house and at 10:16 p.m. the same vehicle slowly passed Jim's house again going east and most likely left the area, but we are checking to see if the same vehicle was captured by any other camera.

I have no idea what they are doing, but they may be taking photos of our homes.

This troubles me. Unfortunately, at 3:32 a.m. this morning, the same vehicle went slowly past Chuck's house heading south and again at 3:35 a.m. heading north. Now it really troubles me. To date, that vehicle has not been captured on any other of our surveillance cameras.

We ran the plate and there is no record of it . We all know that police plates are separated and in a confidential file. I called a friend in the CIA and he ran the plate through the confidential file. No hit. Now we all need to be concerned.

I spoke to the General and Jim before the meeting and they told me that all the resources of WATCH24 are available for our use. I need to tag that vehicle ASAP so we always know where it is. But that will require a WATCH24 agent to be in each of your neighborhoods every hour of every day.

But here is the question I need you to answer. If the vehicle is spotted by us, do we have it followed and after we leave your neighborhood, call for a traffic stop and find out who these idiots are and what they are up to? Or do we have them followed, try to tag the vehicle, and see where they take us? Or do we try to do both, which is risky and we could end up with nothing?"

The conversation that followed included comments from everyone which went from it being a trap to sue us if we violated their rights to, they could be hired assassins and we need to take them off the street.

I finally attempted to end the discussion by saying, "Let's pause for a moment and consider the following. For those of us who worked the streets, we always thought it was foolish and dangerous for a supervisor to start barking orders over the radio while he was sitting at his desk, and we were in the middle of a life and death tactical situation. My favorite one was, 'Don't do anything 'til I get there.' How did we respond? We ignored him or her and did what we had to do take control of the situation. WATCH 24 has an outstanding cadre of professional, well-trained men and women. So, my answer to Joe is that we do not know enough to make that decision. Those type of decisions need to be made by the supervisor at the scene after he or she considers all the information available."

Everyone agreed and Joe spoke again, "If the cameras or anyone spots the car again, I will send a text message to the group. In any case I will update everyone at tomorrow's Zoom meeting."

Jim closed the meeting with, "If no one has a question or a concern that cannot wait for a day, speak up. Hearing none, this meeting has ended."

I love that line. In almost fifty years of meetings, I can count on one hand the number of times that the meeting did not end after that statement.

Once I signed off the computer, I sat there in my study, contemplating exactly how I was going to break this news to Kim. I was quite sure she would say that she was not going through this again and would be leaving home until it was over.

I was only partially correct. Kim's first question was, "Why only our house and Jim's and Patricia's."

"I do not know," I said.

She asked, "Do you think they know where Marie and Jason live?

I responded, "I have no way of knowing that now."

"Okay, after all we have been through, I am going to ask you for a few favors," she began. " I love you and I do not want anything to happen to any of us. First, promise me you will tell me everything just like you did the last time."

"That's a given," I replied, "and I love you too and I am not going to let anyone harm our family."

"Unfortunately, there are no guaranties in life," Kim continued. "I will stay in this house and if nothing happens, fine. But if there is any indication of trouble, I am asking you to move me, Marie, our granddaughter and Patricia to that house in the woods and make sure that we are protected. I will make sure that all of us will be ready to leave with a short notice."

I explained, "We already have it in the plan and the safe house is ready and stocked if needed. The entire safe area has been fortified and in addition to the house, there is a lodge that will house up to thirty more people."

"Let's pray to the Lord that it never comes to that," Kim concluded.

"It is only by risking our persons from one hour to another that we live at all."

—William James

CHAPTER 14

Joe texted all of us early this morning and asked if we could delay the Zoom meeting fifteen minutes, which we did. Tom was on early but left the meeting and returned at 10:20 a.m. and the meeting started.

As planned, Joe gave us an update on the dark blue Jeep.

"The blue Jeep Cherokee has not shown up again on any of our cameras. We have reviewed the last thirty days for all the security cameras with no luck. We have alarmed the system for an alert on a dark 2015 Jeep Cherokee computer match, and we will also physically review all the camera images. Sorry, but currently, we have nothing to add. But Tom has essential information for you.

Tom told us that Assistant Director Peters ran a confidential check through NCIC for any dark colored 2015 Cherokees stolen or involved in a crime for the last six months. He got back a computer sheet with seventy-eight hits which he will give me later this evening."

Tom continued," George also told me that he spoke to Agent Lawson and gave him his personal cell number if he needed to talk to him. AD Peters, who is clearly on our side, is concerned that many of the agents know that the FBI has opened a case and is investigating us. The agents are not exactly sure what is going on, but the rumor is that this case came directly from the Attorney General. It is likely they heard all the radio traffic generated by our digital twins at the Mayflower Hotel. And rest assured, they saw the surveillance vehicle parked near the Mayflower. So, in their eyes, we have been classified as the 'enemy' as evidenced by Agent Lawson who thought he was going after the 'bad guys.'

At the same time, the agents know that they are committing many, shall we say infractions, that they do not want to be discovered, in fear of disciplinary action. The Constitution has been shredded and the oath of office is nothing but a piece of paper. What we have now is an FBI out of control and run amok. I know that it was our intention to create paranoia in the Washington Field Office, and that is exactly what we have accomplished. Now we must find a way to control it before it really gets out of hand. Given our President, this will be difficult, if not impossible."

Changing subjects, Tom continued, "I did not have time to fully review the evidence I received but let me say it is damning and as expected it leads right to the upper echelon of the FBI and the Department of Justice. There are also copies of written requests sent to the Oval Office for approval."

"I have a few thoughts I would like to share," I stated. "As we closed the Zoom meeting yesterday, my thought was that our operation looks more promising that we could really make a difference and return America to some form of normalcy, whatever that is. But my optimism is limited because I truly believe that returning our country to where we were several years ago may be impossible. There are too many areas of our federal government that have deteriorated beyond repair. Let me give you examples. The lack of law and order is everywhere. The President does not obey the law and the politicians do not obey the law. The crime statutes are meaningless to a vast majority of the people because the prosecutors refuse to charge criminals and the judges release violent criminals with little or no bail. Our governments at all levels are trying to defund the police when in reality, their social agenda has already destroyed the police, and no one wants the job anymore. And today, I heard on the news that multiple jurisdictions have not sent their crime statistics to the FBI, as required by the law, for over a year. There are no longer any real accurate crime figures for America. Now the radical socialist politicians can dish out anything they want to the public and the press and no one can hold them accountable.

Will the American people ever trust the federal government again? Probably not in our lifetime.

What are the chances that we will ever substantially reduce our national debt? Slim to none.

Will we be able to restore law and order for all people in all parts of our country? I do not know the answer, but I know it will be difficult and take a long time.

Will we be able to return our military to the best fighting force in the world? I know we have the public support to do it, but we need the leadership to do it.

Did our current President stop Russia from invading Ukraine? No, and the support from the United States for Ukraine was too little and too late.

Will our President unite the free world and hopefully prevent China from invading Taiwan? No, and the attack is eminent.

Can the free world prevent Iran and North Korea from obtaining nuclear weapons without a strong America? I hope so, but right now I can't be sure.

Will the President of the United State again be the leader of the free world? One can hope.

I know this is pessimistic and filled with sarcasm, but I want everyone in America to understand what we are facing and the only way we will bring America back to the nation we can be proud of, is to unite our country and be united in all our efforts."

General Monroe immediately stated, "What Chuck said is all true and is exactly what the American people need to hear if we are ever going to have a functioning democratic republic again. The article that I am about to read was written by the New York Post Issues and Insights Editorial Board and was published today. It is the most accurate, sobering message that I have ever read and likewise, should be read by the entire world:

> *'What would the President be doing differently if his goal were to purposely send the country into a tailspin? He set off a 40-decade-high inflation spiral with his $2 trillion 'rescue' plan, threw open the borders to millions of illegal immigrants and worsened shortages of baby formula and spiking gasoline prices, not to mention 'disastrous Afghanistan retreat.' Each time he claimed to be 'caught off guard,' yet he knew or should have known, what would happen.' So 'how much of a stretch is it' to think it's all about pushing 'to transition' the country into some sort of socialist Nirvana?'*

From where I stand, this is treason, and the President should immediately be impeached."

Judge Walters spoke next, "General, thank you for sharing that article with us. I wish every paper around the world would publish it.

I have been a federal judge for over thirty years and to be honest, I believe the federal justice system is basically useless. Let me back up my statement with a recent event that none of us will ever forget.

The never-ending 'RussiaGate' investigation epitomizes the cliché, 'Justice delayed is justice denied.'

In May of 2017, a former Director of the FBI was appointed as special counsel to take over and expand an existing FBI counterintelligence investigation into possible Russian interference in the 2016 United States elections. Almost two years and thirty-two million dollars later, the report was completed without indictments of the true architects of this fraud.

According to an article in the New York Post on June 11, 2017, 'the RussiaGate scandal was thrust upon the country by the FBI and the former Director. The FBI knew the Trump-Russia collusion narrative was utter bunk even as it suggested otherwise to Congress, the courts and the public early in 2017. Evidence revealed by the present special counsel proves it beyond dispute.'

On October 19, 2020, Special Counsel was appointed by the Attorney General to continue the investigation into the RussiaGate scandal. Twenty months later, there has been two indictments and one conviction and the actual plotters of this scandal have still not been held accountable. If they had been arrested and convicted, we would not be presently witnessing the destruction of America.

In conclusion, after over five years of federal investigations and the expenditure of millions of taxpayers' dollars, the investigation is ongoing and the FBI is still corrupt. I do not want to return to the federal government we used to have and worry about the future of America, I want a new streamlined federal government with term limits for Congress, accountability for the federal law enforcement and intelligence agencies, a strong well-equipped military, a smaller federal bureaucracy without a 'deep state,' and a federal criminal justice system that actually works rather than the inept, ineffective, foot-dragging system we have now.

Chuck, thank you for your earlier comments. All of us do not want to return to the old America, we need to fight for a new, better America."

I would like to add a few final points," Jim said. "Remember years ago, there was a major change in the appointment of the Director of the FBI. The tenure for the appointment was changed to ten years to keep politics out of the Bureau. We can all see how well that worked out. I believe we need to go back to the drawing board.

After some thought, I think it would be smart to postpone our monthly luncheons for now. All of us sitting at a table together in a restaurant is probably not a wise move. I would rather play it safe, than be sorry.

In closing, we all benefited today by our open, candid discussions. Thank you. Let's all stay safe out there, the world has gone crazy."

"The care of human life and happiness, and not their destruction, is the first and only object of good government."
—Thomas Jefferson

CHAPTER 15

There were no updates on Friday and Kim and I had a quiet weekend at home which we needed, to lower our apprehensions. We had a cookout on Saturday and after church on Sunday, we went to one of our favorite restaurants for a nice brunch. What I did notice is that both of us were constantly turning our heads in search of a dark blue Jeep Cherokee or anything we saw that could be threatening.

I did notice that Kim had closed all the blinds or pulled the drapes on all the front windows. And I checked to make sure both our firearms were loaded and in each of our nightstands. This is not how either one of us wanted to live our retirement, but we all know that life has some strange twists.

Jim had to move the Zoom meeting to Tuesday because Patricia had her six-month checkup at 10:00 a.m.

Kim went out on her weekly hunt for baby formula which has

been her obsession since she heard of the shortage. She already has at least a month's supply, boxed and in order by expiration dates. And I know Marie and Jason have a collection as well. What did surprise me is that Sharon also buys baby formula when she sees it. I asked Kim if she thought Sharon was pregnant. She replied, "That would be nice, but neither one of us is going to ask that question. Telling your parents that they are going to be grandparents again is something they will want to tell us together when they are ready. And you better act surprised." And that is exactly what I will do.

I did a little yard work on Monday morning with a rake in my hands and a semiautomatic in my one pocket and my cell phone in the other. When Kim pulled into the garage, I asked her how she made out. "Jackpot," she said with enthusiasm. "There is a case in the trunk with some groceries."

I spent the afternoon in my study, paying bills and going over notes for tomorrow's Zoom meeting. Kim was in the kitchen cooking dinner. When I went into the kitchen for a bottle of water and saw all the food on the counter, I knew exactly what Kim was doing. She was making dinner for at least ten to twelve people. The two of us would have a meal tonight and the remainder would be frozen and ready if we had to go to the safe house. Kim has always been a planner.

After dinner, we sat and watched a movie together. At about 8:50, my cell alerted me that there was a conference call. When I joined the group, Jim checked to make sure everyone was on and stated, "We had a shooting and Tom will give us the details."

Tom began, "At about 8:35 this evening a passing vehicle fired two shots into FBI Agent Mark Lawton's home. The first round pierced Mark's upper left arm. His wife Susan and the baby were not injured. As he was grabbing his service weapon, he called 911 from his home phone and once the dispatcher had the information she needed, Mark called Assistant Director George Peters on his cell phone. On his way to Mark's home, George called me to advise me of the shooting. I asked him how we could help. He told me that the FBI would handle the attempted homicide of their agent, but he will call me as soon as he can. So now we are just waiting for an update."

Jim said. "There is plenty we can do. Joe, make sure the safe house is ready for a crowd. Ben and Carol, who you all know, are already heading that way. Chuck, ask Kim and Marie if they could help Susan with the baby at the safe house and I will ask Patricia to help also."

What Jim just did was move our families to the safe house without alarming them that their lives may be in danger. And I know that Kim, Marie and I will be much more relaxed knowing they are safe.

Jim continued, "Joe put security and surveillance systems in Mark's and George's homes. And get George set up with a laptop and one of our phones so he can attend the Zoom meetings and be available for conference calls.

Tom, fill George in on our plans and have him tell his wife that Susan is going to need her help at the safe house. Do you know her first name?"

"No." Tom said. "But I will get it to you ASAP."

Jim went on, "Judge, General, and Tom, tell your families to get ready to be moved to the safe house. I am not taking any chances. One more incident and everybody is going." And knowing Joe has been divorced for years, Jim added, "Joe, if you currently have a significant other, she is welcome also."

Joe has a profound sense of humor, and his response helped lighten the moment, "Jim, can I bring more than one?"

After the laughter stopped, he added, "Only kidding. I am in a dry spell right now and I will be too busy to spend time in the safe house. And if you see me there more than an occasional evening, we are all in deep trouble." And he meant it.

Jim ended the conference call by saying, "We will need updates from everyone at tomorrow's Zoom meeting. Stay alert."

Within a minute of hanging up, my phone rang again. It was Jim.

"Chuck, I just wanted to let you know that I am giving special assignments to Tom and Sharon. I am sending Tom to the hospital to be with Mark and his family. I asked Tom to talk to Mark and if he has any doubts about staying in the FBI, I want Tom to suggest that he should consider a career in WATCH24.

I need Sharon to take care of Kim, Marie, Katherine, and Patricia and bring them to the safe house early tomorrow morning. I do not want any of them to go through anything close to what they experienced twelve years ago. And I know you and I will feel much better knowing our families are safe."

And the conversation ended with me saying, "Thank you."

I know that Jim has always regretted that he did not move Patricia out of their home during the Sanchez investigation. He had suggested to Patricia that she should go to the safe house, but she declined saying, "I will stay right here with you. We will be fine." Unfortunately, they were not and with Patricia in a wheelchair, Jim went into action. I cannot tell you how many times he has said, "Never again."

Jim's first project was to make the WATCH24 safe house handicapped accessible. But that wasn't enough for Jim. Next thing we knew, Jim was signing a contract to build a sixteen-room lodge with a large full kitchen, a huge dining area, a den, a recreation/exercise room, and a new security office. Joe spent months on the site designing and installing an updated security system that puts Fort Knox to shame.

On Tuesday morning, everyone was online and ready to go fifteen minutes before starting time, so Jim began by welcoming FBI Assistant Director George Peters to the Zoom. "Glad to see you aboard George, I hope you are not sitting in your FBI office."

George replied, "No, I am in my home study with the door closed per Joe's instructions. And thank you for including me in such an elite group."

Jim commented, "Not considered elite by everyone, as you will soon learn.

And Joe, you amaze me, I did not expect George to be with us until Thursday. Excellent job. George, why don't we start by you giving us an update."

George started, "First and foremost, Mark, Susan and their baby, Dawn are all doing fine and still at the hospital. Mark is lucky. The bullet took a large chunk out of his left upper arm and the doctor told me he should have a full recovery. Tom told me about your offer to move Mark and his family to the safe house and they are ready to go. I would like to always have one Agent with them. I assigned Agent Bill Holland, the son of one of my life-long friends, and I have complete trust in him. He is one of the 'good guys' and as sharp as they come and will be promoted soon. I understand that he cannot bring any electronics with him, but

Joe told me he could give him a secure phone if you approve it."

Jim interjected, "Does anyone have any concerns or questions on George's request?" After a short silence, Jim stated, "Approved."

Joe added, "That's great since Bill's new phone is in my vehicle and already programmed. If you look at your phone later, you will see his name and number in your directory."

George was a bit shocked and stated, "This group is amazing; with twenty plus years in the Bureau, I have never seen the FBI move this fast."

General Monroe spoke up, "And you never will. Remember, it is the federal government."

George continued, "I explained all of this to my wife, Diane and she feels so bad for the Lawton family, that she would like to go the safe house and help as much as possible."

"Great," Jim said, "tell her to start packing."

"The crime scene did not give us much evidence. Mark said there were two shots. One bullet was recovered from a wall in the home, and it could have been the one that broke the window and struck Mark. It appears to be a nine-millimeter, but we will have better information after the forensic lab completes their examination. There were no shell casings found and I imagine they are in the perpetrator's vehicle. I made a copy of the report and all the photographs for Tom to review and hold as evidence for the grand jury and trials," George said.

"We canvassed the neighborhood for cameras and found one on a home on Mark's street, about a block and a half away. After reviewing the images, it looks like a dark, unknown color Jeep SUV was heading toward Mark's home about the same time the shots were fired. We could not see any plates. The forensic unit is at that home now, and when I get more information, I will send a text message. I am signing off now and heading to the office. Thank you for your trust and including me in your meeting. I am a bit more optimistic than I have been in months and I will not let you down."

Tom told Jim that his wife, Donna decided to visit her sister, who she has not seen in over a year, and when she returns, they will make a decision on the safe house. Both the General and the Judge stated for now they feel quite safe at home but are ready to make the move if necessary.

Jim concluded the meeting by saying that we all had "a lot on our plate" right now, so we should be ready to discuss case updates and any items of interest at Thursday's meeting.

"It is the tragedy of the world that no one knows what he doesn't know—and the less a man knows, the more sure he is that he knows everything."

—Joyce Cary

CHAPTER 16

When I told Kim to start packing for her trip to the safe house, she told me she was already packed and smiled.

"Is Marie packed also?" I asked.

With that same smile, she replied. "Of course."

When I told her Sharon would be picking them up, her smile got larger. When I added that Patricia was going with them also, the smile disappeared and she said, "I am happy that Patricia is going, but obviously this has gotten much more serious since we last talked."

"I am not certain yet, but a camera picked up a dark Jeep Cherokee on the same street where the FBI Agent was shot last night," I told her. "In fact, Special Agent Mark Lawton, his wife Susan and their new baby Dawn are also heading to the safe house. And, by the way, Ben and Carol will be there also."

The smile returned to her face and she said, "Sounds like a reunion; I can't wait to see them again. Now all I must worry about is you and Tom."

"You will see Tom at the safe house this afternoon," I said. "He is driving the Lawton family there. And don't worry about us. If Sharon is away, Tom will stay in the guest room so he will be closer to the WATCH24 Headquarters."

Kim ended with, "Good, I better call Marie."

I went to my study and called Tom Wilson for an update. I began by asking him if he needed any help with the evidence. He told me that what first appeared to be a duplicate, was the same information from two diverse sources which will add credence to the evidence. He said he had his own way of matching evidence to an event and a person, so for right now, it was a job for a single pair of eyes.

We also had a lengthy discussion whether the shooting was an attempted murder or was someone trying to send Mark a message. Gangs often use this method to send messages for 'correcting behavior.' Most murders or attempted murders have a hell of a lot more lead flying through the air. If the blinds were shut, I lean toward a message. If the blinds were open, I could not really say. Tom agreed.

I then asked Tom if the FBI Forensic Unit was going to return to see if they can find the second bullet.

He replied, "I think so. But right now, they have made that camera a priority and rightfully so. If they do not return, we will look for it."

I ended the conversation saying that since we are both going to be old bachelors for a while, we should grab an occasional lunch or dinner, if it is before 6:00 p.m. He added, "Make that 5:00 p.m." And we both chuckled.

A brief time later, Sharon arrived to pick up Kim for the trip to the safe house. As we were saying our goodbyes, Kim, with tears in her eyes, gave me a written list of the frozen meals she had prepared for me, with the exact instruction for heating them. That's my wife—thoughtful and organized. After telling me to be careful numerous times, Sharon and Kim headed out to pick up Marie, Katherine, and Patricia.

I stood in the doorway as the SUV pulled out of the driveway, frozen in the thought of how crazy this world has become. I try to stay positive, but I still have that sinking feeling that America has declined so far since this President had taken office, that I do not see how we will ever recover. I know it is all in the Lord's hands, but watching your family walk out the door of your home, because you are not sure you can protect them, is devastating.

When it was time for dinner, I took out the list Kim had given me, drew a line through the first meal, because I knew they were stacked in the freezer in perfect order as listed.

I just finished cleaning up. when my cell indicated I had a text message. It was from Joe telling me there would be a Zoom meeting with my family at 7:00 p.m. and he included the code for the meeting.

That's Joe. He is certainly one of the best electronic technicians in the world, but more importantly, he is a kind, thoughtful person who never misses a chance to make life better for all of us.

When I logged into the meeting, my whole family was there, except for Jason, who was at his home in Virginia Beach. The next fifteen minutes lifted my spirits and everyone seemed happy to be together in a safe environment. Tom told me that there was a WATCH24 agent staying with Jason and that he would be staying in our guest room tonight and arriving sometime between 10:00 and 10:15 p.m. As the call ended, I heard, a single "be careful" in unison from everyone.

When Tom arrived, we sat at the kitchen table and we each had a beer.

Tom told me that Jason offered Bob, the WATCH24 agent, their guest room and he thought that put Jason more at ease.

Tom also said that he really liked Mark Lawton and his family. I asked him if Mark was going to stay with the FBI. Mark indicated that he wanted to talk to Tom about the future, but Tom thought the day after he was shot was too soon.

We discussed the shooting case for the next twenty minutes and I brought him up to date to include my earlier discussion with Tom Wilson. By 11:00 p.m., we were both in bed.

I had coffee, cereal and pastries ready by the time Tom got to the kitchen. As we were eating, he told me that he spoke to Sharon this morning and she was going to spend one more day there to help everyone get organized. Currently Ben, Carol and Sharon are staying in the lodge and everyone else is in the safe house. Sharon is going to offer the Lawtons a large room in the lodge so they have more privacy.

By 7:30 a.m., Tom was off to work and I went to my study to prepare for tomorrow's Zoom meeting. In my mind, I had several events I wanted to discuss and I wanted to get them on paper. I give George Peters a tremendous amount of credit for working with our group and at the same time, after the shooting at Mark's home, I am very much concerned for his safety.

And since we have no real leads on the dark blue Jeep Cherokee, I am relieved that his wife, Diane is at the safe house.

"What good is it for someone to gain the whole world, yet forfeit their soul?"

—Mark 8:36

CHAPTER 17

Our Thursday morning Zoom meeting started with Jim telling us that Joe was someplace in the world installing a surveillance camera and would most likely not make the meeting, but he had promised that if he had any hot information, he would send a text to all of us.

First on the agenda was an update on the Lawton shooting investigation.

George opened with an announcement, "We have created a Task Force for this case. I spoke to the Sheriff yesterday afternoon and he has agreed to add two detectives to help us.

Mark, Susan and Dawn are all doing well at the safe house thanks to Jim and Mark's next medical appointment is in two weeks.

The lab was able to slightly enhance the video from the neighbor's security camera, but we are still unable to identify anyone in the vehicle or get a readable plate number.

The National Crime Information Center staff is still working on the list of stolen Jeep Cherokees and has been reduced to about half. No leads to date.

And the forensic unit is at Mark's home again this morning looking for the bullet from the second shot. Nothing yet. I will keep you updated."

"Chuck, you are next," Jim said.

"I have three items I want to discuss with you today," I began.

"Another pro-life organization has been attacked, this time in Minnesota. The office of Minnesota Citizens Concerned for Life, the state National Right to Life affiliate, was vandalized with spray paint and its windows were broken. This is the latest in at least sixty attacks against pro-life organizations nationwide since the draft opinion overturning *Roe v. Wade* was leaked.

According to news reports, the White House is holding emergency meetings to figure out what to do if the draft opinion holds as the Supreme Court's final decision in the Dobbs case. One option reportedly under consideration is to declare a "national public health emergency."

That would be a very strange action. It would be the first public health emergency ever declared by an American government whose purpose is to ensure that 1 in 5 babies continues to be aborted. In other words, it would be a public health emergency to guarantee more death.

I am still very much troubled with the continuous unconstitutional, corrupt actions of the FBI. I still believe that most of the agents are good, honest individuals, but I also see the corruption cancer growing throughout the Bureau.

The recent events surrounding the President's daughter's diary surfacing after she left it in her room at a rehab center is troubling. The FBI evidently adopted a case on this. I am not sure there is any crime here, but I am damn sure that there is no federal crime here. I understand that there may have been entries in the diary that may be embarrassing to the family, but that certainly does not justify the President to use the FBI as his own secret police and the Director should have never assigned the case for investigation. No wonder the American public has lost its trust in the FBI.

And my third item is by far the most serious and could easily destroy America.

In May 2013, our President, who was then Vice President, helped arrange a Memorandum of Understanding with Communist China allowing its corporations to have privileged access to United States stock and bond markets. This deal allowed China to be exempt from compliance with American laws and regulations designed to protect investors from fraudulent and bankrupt companies.

In December of 2013, the Vice President and his son flew in Air Force Two to Beijing, China where they met with China's BHR Capital executives and left with a 10 percent equity stake in BHR. Over the next several years, they expanded their deals with other additional Communist China companies which resulted in the President's family receiving millions of dollars from China.

Fast forward to today, and we have China boasting that it plans to conquer Taiwan and all we get from the White House is lip service despite the threats China is making against the United States. This is what happens when our President is weak and corrupt. Now let me explain what America will be facing in the near future.

Taiwan manufactures 65 percent of the world's semiconductors and 92 percent of the world's advanced semiconductors which are needed for almost everything in the modern world—vehicles, planes, military weapons, computers, phones, communication systems, power grids, industrial equipment and so much more.

The reason the price of used vehicles has increased so dramatically and new cars are so difficult to find in the United States, is the shortage of semiconductors.

I am not alone in predicting that Communist China will invade Taiwan before the mid-term elections, in fear that a majority change in the Senate would result in the removal of an extremely weak President for a stronger one that China cannot control. And if China conquers Taiwan, this will trigger a strategically disastrous, global dependency on Communist China for semiconductors and the America we love and cherish will be changed forever. And China's quest is to replace the Unites States as the most powerful country in the world. And this is the path they have chosen.

Gentlemen, this is what we are up against, and we should be broadcasting it daily to America and the world. And if we can come together and unite against China, Russia, North Korea, and Iran, we just may save the world."

General Monroe added, "We have known for years that this day would come. Year after year, President after President, no one wanted to deal with the problem and chose to kick the can down the road to the next administration. From 2017 to 2020, we started to make progress in this area and America became energy independent for the first time in many years which improved America's standing. I really do not care what political party you belong to, whether you are a liberal or a conservative, or if you liked or disliked our last President. It is critical that we all stand together and rescue our country."

And the Judge added, "And bring back law and order to America."

Jim said, "Chuck, you are right, we need to broadcast that the problems Americans are facing will impact the entire free world and must be attacked globally. Unfortunately, that is not how our President views it.

I would like to suggest to each of you that you write an editorial in your field of expertise that emphasizes what we need to save our country and the free world. Each one of you will pass your editorial to everyone in the group for input and comments. Make your changes and/or additions and send your completed editorial along with a short biography on another piece of paper to me. It will be my responsibility to make sure that they are widely published throughout America and beyond.

One final thought. As most of you know, the WATCH24 safe house is now a safety compound with a house and a sixteen-bedroom lodge which together can easily accommodate forty people. We expanded it because safety is our highest priority in this crazy world. After much thought and reflection, I wanted us to never forget those who gave so much during the Sanchez investigation. The Patricia House and the Steven Oates Memorial Lodge will forever remind us of the sacrifice made by my wife, who never complains, and the ultimate sacrifice paid by Steve, our good friend. May he rest in peace."

There was about ten seconds of silence followed by loud applause.

After the meeting, I did the household chores I inherited

when Kim went to the safe house. I was rather surprised to find that Tom left the guest room and guest bath perfectly clean and to be honest, his mother deserves the credit. Kim tells me I still do not know how to properly make a bed and she is right.

After a small lunch, I headed to my study. Being a workaholic, I always completed my tasks before taking time to relax. With everything that is taking place, I knew there was something I should be doing, but right now I do not know what that is. I never liked idle time and was hoping the phone would ring or I would get a text message, or anything that would give me direction. Ten minutes later I got my wish and received a call from Tom Wilson.

I answered and Tom said, "The FBI Forensic Unit left Mark's home about an hour ago. They did not find any further evidence, and no bullet."

"Did they check everything including the eaves and the roof?" I asked.

"The supervisor said they did, but to be certain, I went over to Mark's house with my own ladder and walked the entire roof. Nothing," Tom said.

I closed with, "Thanks for letting me know." And I ended the call.

Now I have something to do. I took a clean pad and drew a line right down the center. On the left side I wrote, "Attempted Murder." On the right side I wrote, "Unknown Warning Message." Then I got to work.

About 3:00 p.m., I went to the freezer and took out the next two meals that Kim had prepared. I thought I would give Tom his choice since Sharon was coming home tomorrow and this would be the last night that he would use the guest room.

I worked in the study for another hour and then moved to the family room to watch the news. It was a normal day. Chicago had ten shooting with two dead; New York City had four shootings with two dead; Philadelphia had three shootings with one dead; And Washington, DC had two shootings. There were smash and grabs throughout the country, too many armed robberies to count and at least twenty violent felons released to the streets with no bail or low bail. Welcome to the newest Banana Republic!

Tom came through the door right at 6:00 p.m. I put two beers on the kitchen table and we both sat down for a father/son talk which was in reality a son/father talk since he had more information to share than I did. We eventually got to the Lawton investigation and after looking at everything, we agreed, in our minds, that it was a "warning message."

I asked, "How is Mark doing?"

Tom replied, "They are all doing fine. But I am not sure that Susan wants Mark to go back to the FBI."

I concluded with, "Let Mark know that Joe really likes him and wants him to come work for WATCH24."

"The spirit of resistance to government is so valuable on certain occasions, that I wish it to be always kept alive. It will often be exercised when wrong, but better so than not to be exercised at all."
—Thomas Jefferson

CHAPTER 18

We had a great dinner and afterward, the conversation centered around our family, looking at the future. Tom told me that he and Sharon were talking about starting a family. Kim would be so proud of me. I followed her orders, I bit my tongue, and did not ask any questions. But I do think Tom was setting me up for big news at a later time.

At 8:45 p.m., my cell phone toned that I had a text message. When I picked up my phone, I realized it was an emergency message from George Peters:

"Several shots were just fired at my home. Front window shattered. No one hurt. FBI and Sheriff en route. More to follow."

"Another shooting at George Peters home. No injuries," I told Tom.

I was getting another emergency text message from Joe.

"Confirmed by camera. Dark blue Jeep Cherokee in the area."

At the same time, Tom was reading a text on his phone. He said, "I gotta go. They want to saturate the area around the shooting scene to see if we can get eyes on the Jeep Cherokee."

Not exactly the way I want to end dinner. I sat there for a few minutes and thought, the time is close to the time of the Lawton shooting, it appears to be the same vehicle, both targets were FBI homes, and only a few shots were fired at both locations.

Now I am almost sure these shootings are "warning messages" and not attempted murders. Then I realized that whoever is in that Jeep knows where both Jim and I live. Why the FBI agents and not us? Evidently, they do not consider our group as a threat, yet they view the FBI as a threat. But a threat to whom. I do not think it has anything to do with dirty bombs. But it may have much to do about dirty cops, especially if they believe Mark and George are informants or whistleblowers.

I called Tom Wilson and let him know my thoughts. He also thought these were warning messages, but doubted it was in any way tied to the FBI. I told him that I hoped he was correct, but thought he rejected FBI participation too early. I told him that I know that is a hard pill to swallow, but reminded him that in the Sanchez case, the bad guy was the Secret Service Assistant Special Agent-in-Charge of the White House Detail and I was his boss.

He then said, "Thanks for the reminder; you are right, and I withdraw that last statement I made. We need to examine these shootings from every possible angle."

It was almost two hours later before George found the time to make a private call to our group.

He stated by saying, "I do not see very much difference between tonight's shooting and the Lawton shooting with the exception that Mark caught a bullet in his arm and I was lucky. I heard two shots, but it appears only one bullet entered the house. But we will not know for sure until tomorrow when the forensic unit can look at everything in the sunlight. And I do not think it was a coincidence that both shootings were at about 8:35 p.m. We also believe these were warning shots with no intention of killing anyone. However, a charge of discharging a firearm into an occupied dwelling will be a life sentence. "

"One could hope," added Judge Walters.

"I am certainly glad that Diane went to the safe house," Jim said to George. "She needs to stay there until we arrest this crew and clean up this mess. When she does return home, the new security system should reassure her that she will be safe in her own home. Remember, Patricia and Kim have already been through this and can help her make the adjustment.

George, I assume the FBI will put addition surveillance on your home, but WATCH24 will be increasing the surveillance on our homes as well."

George said, "One more thing I have to say. Kudos to Joe for his placement of that surveillance camera which immediately captured the Jeep and the plate number."

And always humble Joe responded, "That was one of the easiest installs I have made in a long time."

And every one of us knew that was a lie.

I heard Tom unlock the front door and head straight for the guest room at 2:10 a.m. I think it best to let him sleep in the morning.

At 6:00 a.m., I was already up, sitting at the kitchen table with my second cup of coffee and reading the morning paper. It is depressing and further evidence that America is in deep trouble, when you read the headlines:

"Food Prices Expected to Increase by 17 percent by Year's End."

"The President is the drug cartel's Best Friend."

"Five major US cities already on track to break their 2021 homicide totals."

"Are we witnessing the slaughter of the American way of life?"

"Three People Stabbed on Ocean City Boardwalk."

"Border Patrol nabs 15 people on terror watch list in record-breaking May."

And the winner for the day comes from the United Kingdom and serves as proof that the entire world has gone crazy:

"Male blood donor, 66, required to state on form if he's pregnant—part of new, woke UK policy. He's turned away from clinic when he refuses to answer."

You can't make this stuff up!

To my surprise, Tom was up by 7:00 a.m. We went over every aspect of last night's shooting while we ate our eggs and bacon. Tom was looking forward to Sharon coming home and everything returning to normal.

I corrected him saying, "We are a long way from normal."

He replied, "Touché, you are so right." He thanked me for breakfast and left for work.

Since unsecure cell phones are not allowed in or near the

compound, I called Ben and asked him to give his phone to Kim so we could talk. I am certain that Ben knew exactly why I was calling and he told me it may take a short while to find her, but he would find a place where she could speak in private. I thanked him and waited.

I was expecting the question. Kim immediately said, "Hon, is everything all right?"

"Kim, everything is fine," I said. "I just want to bring you up to date, as promised."

"Good, thanks" she said. "What's up?"

I took my time and gave her a summary of the shooting last night and included that we all think it was a warning message and not an attempted homicide. The only question she asked was, "Are there going to be more shootings?"

I told Kim that I really did not know, but we have a WATCH24 agent around our homes every night. I told her that when Tom's wife returns from visiting her sister, she is going to the safe compound. Kim thought that was the right thing to do and said she would welcome her when she arrived. We spoke for a few more minutes and she thanked me again for updating her.

It was almost noon before George initiated the conference call to give us the results of the search and said, "Good morning. The forensic unit just left my home and I have the window company coming in fifteen minutes to replace my shattered windowpane. I can be brief because I do not have much to pass on. We searched for hours looking for evidence of a second slug. We found absolutely nothing. I am at a loss for words, except to say, there is something very strange about these two shooting. My best guess is that none of us has ever seen a case like this in all our years in law enforcement. I did talk to Diane this morning and let her know that everything is okay. Are there any questions?"

Steve asked, "Looking at all of this in its entirety, do you think there is a possibility that someone in the FBI is involved in this?"

George responded, "I am not making any accusations, but we would be remiss if we did not consider the FBI could be involved."

Sadly, everyone agreed.

"Out of this nettle, danger, we pluck this flower, safety."
　　—Shakespeare

CHAPTER 19

Early Saturday morning I got a phone call from Jim. "Chuck, let me tell you what I am doing today," Jim began. "With the number of people we have at the safe compound and the probability that more will head that way, I thought we should have a medical professional present, especially with a baby and your pregnant daughter being there. WATCH24 has a contract with a Physician's Assistant, Ann Smith, who is a wonderful person with twenty years of medical experience. I am flying to Culpeper in a helicopter to pick her up and bring her to the compound. Join us and we can surprise our wives, your daughter and granddaughter. It will also give us time to talk and figure out what in the hell is going on with these shootings."

I replied, "Thanks, Jim. I would like that."

And Jim said, "I thought you would. The helicopter is at WATCH24 headquarters and the vehicle to bring you here will be in your driveway in twenty minutes. You better get ready."

That's one thing about Jim that you had to admit. He is full of surprises, and history has shown that sometimes, those surprises are life changing.

I was able to get ready in twenty minutes and as I was walking out the door, my son, Tom, was pulling in the driveway. "I thought you were off today," I said as I opened the car door. "Everyone is working today, including Sharon," he responded. "We have someone assigned to watch every one of our homes, just in case the Jeep operator decides to take a ride by," Tom stated.

Although it was largely work related, Tom and I had a good discussion. I told him that after giving it much thought last night, I decided to try and get a copy of the White House visitors log for the last ninety days. I know it has been several years since I retired as the Director of the Secret Service, but hoped I still had friends that could covertly help me out. Tom also thought that was a promising idea.

Jim was standing next to the helicopter as we pulled up to the helipad. Within ten minutes we were in the air en route to Culpeper.

It only took me a brief time to see that Jim was accurate when he said that Ann Smith was a "wonderful person," and I would add a "true professional" also. I was impressed.

Ann got right down to business and asked Jim for the names of all people at the compound to include WATCH24 staff and anything she should know about their medical conditions. Jim reached in his folder and handed her the list of names. I gave Ann all the information I had on Kim, Marie and Katherine, and Jim updated Ann on Patricia's condition.

Ann said, "That's a good start, but I will be interviewing and completing an examination of everyone on the first few days."

Jim added, "We have a medical room in the lodge that is well equipped and stocked with medical supplies. Ann, please look it over and if you find anything missing or anything you need or want, give the list to Ben and we will have it for you ASAP."

We circled the compound before we set down, and, although there had been many upgrades and changes, my mind flashed back twelve years to the time we spent there and the relief we felt knowing we were safe.

As we were landing, I saw Ben and Carol standing next to the helipad with two All -Terrain vehicles. Ben took Jim and me to the house and Carol took Ann and her luggage to the lodge.

As we walked through the door, Jim said, "Welcome to the Patricia House. I was going to put a nice picture of my wife on the wall in the foyer, but, as you know, she hates the limelight, and nixed it. I never brought it up again.

As I looked around, I could immediately see that Jim went far beyond simple handicap modifications. It looked better than any inn I have ever seen.

The first voice I heard was Marie's yelling, "Dad is here!"

What a warm feeling that gives you. And quickly, Jim and I were surrounded by people wanting to greet us but wondering why we were there. I hugged Marie and Katherine and Kim immediately kissed me asking if everything was okay. I saw her relief when I said, "Yes."

Jim stood behind Patricia's wheelchair with his hands on her shoulders and explained why we were there and that he and I wanted to surprise our families.

Patricia added, "And that you did."

We all sat down and FBI Agent Mark Lawton introduced himself, his wife, Susan and baby Dawn to Jim and me and thanked Jim for keeping his family safe. FBI Agent Bill Holland followed by also introducing himself.

Jim had already let Carol know that we would be staying for lunch and at noon, Ben, Carol and Ann joined us. Once we were all seated, Jim and Ann stood, Jim introduced Ann and she immediately put everyone at ease and explained how she would help them become one of the "healthiest groups" in America.

After lunch Jim, Patricia, Kim, Ann, and I left and Ben and Carol used the ATVs to transport us to the lodge.

When we opened the door and walked in, I was shocked and said, "Wow, this is not a lodge, this is a five-star hotel."

Jim laughed and said, "Look at it this way, if we ever fully retire, or if the world 'goes to hell in a hand basket,' we can all safely live here and await the rapture. And that may be closer than we think."

Jim pointed to the wall and as I turned my head, I was looking at a picture of Steve Oates in a heavy frame. Underneath this picture it read:

IN MEMORY OF SPECIAL AGENT STEVEN OATES

GREATER LOVE HAS NO ONE THAN THIS,
THAT HE LAY DOWN HIS LIFE FOR HIS FRIENDS.
May he rest in peace in the presence of our God Almighty.

We took a tour of the lodge and you could easily tell that much effort went into its design, detail and decorations. It really was a five-star hotel.

When we viewed the medical room, Ann told Jim that on her

initial look, she did not see anything that she needed and told him that this was better than many of the hospitals where she has worked.

Jim has always taken pride in his work and it shows in his public service and even more so in his private ventures. Jim created the concept of WATCH24, which was much more than the average security firm. The Sanchez case was a worldwide story that propelled WATCH 24 into the multimillion-dollar corporation it is today with contracts all over the free world and almost 2,000 employees. And having known Jim for years, Jim's success is due to his genuine care for people.

The flight home gave us time to candidly discuss the shooting cases in private. I asked rhetorically, "Why are the FBI Agent homes being shot up and not ours. They know where you and I live. What are the "warning messages" trying to stop or prevent? Why two shots and only one bullet enters the home? What is the relevance of 8:35 p.m.?

I told Jim that I would like to look at the White House visitor log for at least the last ninety days.

Jim thought that was a good idea because there is no doubt in his mind that all the direction is coming from the Oval Office. But the question that all of us are striving to answer is, who is really running the country? No one thinks it is the President. Cognitively, he is failing and without a teleprompter, he has difficulty putting sentences together.

I added that another problem for us is that this administration ignores the Constitution, the laws, the rules, the regulations and long-established procedures. And if the bosses ignore them, it is difficult to hold anyone else accountable. In the end, the employees are committing numerous violations with impunity. Look at the FBI, for example. And the fallout from that means that any records we review or subpoena are false or incomplete because no one really cares. I have already heard that the White House visitor logs are incomplete and there are too many exemptions. So, the logs may be useless. We have a federal government that has run amok.

Jim responded that he saw no other choice. We need to keep digging until we turn over the one rock that puts us on the path that exposes everything and gives control back to those who love their country instead of those who only care about lining their pockets.

I told Jim, "Now that we are done, we need to get off our soapboxes before the helicopter lands." And we both laughed.

Tom drove me back to the house, dropped me off and headed home. They did not have much time together this week, so Tom was taking Sharon to her favorite restaurant this evening. And I am still awaiting the news that I am going to be a grandfather again. But as I think about it, I realize that with everything that has happened this week, it is not a suitable time to celebrate. That's okay, I can wait.

I am not that hungry since I ate more for lunch than I normally do. I ate a few crackers with cheese, watched the news and then opened the mail. That was enough for one day. And I went to bed.

My phone woke me up just before 2:00 in the morning letting me know there was a text message. It was a group message from George:

"Earlier this evening, Washington Metro Police responded to a vehicle fire in an alley. Apparently, an SUV vehicle was doused with gasoline and torched. It is now a hunk of charred metal and it was several hours before the PD realized this could be our dark blue Jeep Cherokee. They called the FBI and the FBI Forensic Unit was on the scene at 12:35 a.m. The forensic supervisor just called me and told me he believes this is the Jeep Cherokee involved in the two shootings. I will initiate a conference call sometime around 10:00 this morning with an update."

It took me a while to get back to sleep because, in my mind, I could not determine if this was good or unwelcome news.

I woke up at 7:10 a.m., which surprised me since I am usually up between 5:30 and 6:00 a.m. I made quick decision. I have time to get up, get dressed and make it to early church. And after church, I will treat myself to a full breakfast at my favorite diner. And that is exactly what I did and I was back home by 9:30 a.m.

True to his word, George's conference call began at 10:05 a.m.

"Good morning, I am sorry I disturbed your sleep earlier this morning," George began. "The one piece of evidence I wanted immediately was the Vehicle Identification Number. That's going to have to wait until tomorrow. The forensic unit has a partial VIN, but the vehicle will have to be towed to the FBI Academy where it will be garaged and the lab can work to restore the entire VIN. That will make it easier to determine ownership.

The license plate that was on the vehicle and captured at least twice by Joe's surveillance cameras is missing and a thorough search of the area proved negative.

There were no visible public or private cameras in the alley. Tomorrow, FBI agents from the Washington Field Office will canvass the entire neighborhood and see if we can get any further information.

There was no other physical evidence found in the vehicle due to the intensity of the fire.

However, there is one piece of information that I found interesting. The call to the 911 center came from a cell phone at exactly 8:35 p.m. It appears the cell phone was a throw away most likely purchased at a 7-11 store. We will be following up on that tomorrow as well.

Any questions or comments?"

I spoke immediately, "Obviously, these idiots have carefully timed everything to occur at 8:35 p.m. Why? And what is the significance of these three numbers. It could be related to a badge or shield number of someone they despise, or it could relate to a house or apartment number, or hotel room number or a telephone number, or the number of a store. There are hundreds of possibilities. Think about this today and write down any ideas or thoughts you have and we can discuss it during our Zoom meeting tomorrow."

Jim spoke up, "Why didn't the FBI agents who were working today do the neighborhood canvass?"

George was quick with a response. "Jim, you worked for the FBI for years, you know the answer to that."

And everyone had a laugh.

I thought long and hard on those three numbers: eight, three, five. I even Googled all the variations of the three digits. The results surprised me:

835

Angel number 835 carries a sign and message of independence, self-realization, and manifestation, which could answer most of life's questions. The meaning of 835 is also associated with love and the importance of love in life. Love is the answer to every situation, and we all know that love makes the world a better place.

853

21 US Code § 853 - Criminal forfeitures of property

583

IRS Publication 583 (01/2021), Starting a Business and Keeping Records

538

https://projects.fivethirtyeight.com > President-approval-rating

385

Angel number 385 love the hard work and stubbornness of fours, imitate them. Both numbers are proud and a little lonely. In controversial issues, the number 385 will crush 4 with its authority and the relationship will come to naught.

358

The .358 Winchester is a .35 caliber rifle cartridge based on a necked up .308 Winchester created by Winchester in 1955. The cartridge is also known in Europe as the 9.1x51mm.

And if you use the corresponding letters of the alphabet, you get "HCE," which when googled gives you" highly compensated employee."

As the saying goes, "This is above my pay grade."

The FBI has professionally trained behavioral scientists and my recommendation to George is to send all this information to them.

I spent the rest of my afternoon preparing for the part of tomorrow's meeting that has nothing to do with the number "835". I felt much more productive in my own comfort zone.

Since I had a full breakfast this morning, I had decided to skip lunch. I was now hungry and went to the freezer, took the next frozen meal off the top of the pile, disregarded any thought of leaving it on the counter to thaw, added more time on the microwave and washed my hands for dinner. It tasted the same to me.

I spent the evening with the Sunday paper and was in bed by 10:00 p.m.

"The law has become paralyzed, and there is no justice in the courts. The wicked far outnumber the righteous, so that justice has become perverted."

—Habakkuk 1:4

CHAPTER 20

We are a punctual group and the Monday morning Zoom meeting started on time.

George began the meeting. "It is too early for an update, but the agents are presently canvassing the neighborhood and the lab is working to restore the VIN number, since the dash VIN plate is missing. As soon as I know anything further, I will text it to each of you. Who wants to start the discussion on 835?"

Foolishly, I said, "I will. Let me start by saying after spending hours with this yesterday afternoon, I have more questions and no answers. Let me explain. I first matched letters to the number which resulted gave me "HCE." I have no idea what that could stand for. When I googled it, I got "Highly Compensated Employee." Then I took every variation of 853 and googled each one of them. I did not expect to get much, but I was wrong. 835

is the number of the angel associated with love; 853 is the United States Code number for Criminal forfeitures; 583 is the IRS Publication for Starting a Business and Keeping Records; 538 is a project to measure President approval ratings; 385 is an angel who is stubborn, proud and a little lonely; and 358 is a Winchester .35 caliber rifle cartridge. I kid you not. Look it up.

My recommendation is that we give all of this to the FBI behavioral scientists to figure out. And we spend our time looking for any associations with telephone numbers; the badges or shields of law enforcement personnel; house, store, room, or prison cell numbers or anything any of you want to add."

Jim suggested, "Chuck and George will manage this aspect of the investigation so if you have anything, please let them know. Next, we will talk about the state of America and I know the General wants to share a bit of information with us.

General Monroe said, "I wish I could take the credit for writing this short article I am about to read, but it was written by Matthew Syed, published in this month's NEWSMAX magazine and is an appropriate comment on why America has become so weak."

"While Xi Jinping was resetting the world order through his Belt and Road Initiative and Vladimir Putin was re-creating the Russian empire by annexing Georgia and Crimea, we were arguing over gender-neutral toilets."

The General commented, "How true!"

"And there is one more current policy of this administration that keeps me awake at night and I need to get off my chest. I spent forty years serving and fighting for the America I love and there was not one day that I was not proud of all the men and women in military service. Sadly, I am unable to say that today.

"The West Point cadets are being taught about "whiteness," "race privilege" and other elements of a program, called "Critical Race Theory (CRT), according to documents recently handed over by the military academy. The documents, which include slides, course outlines and emails, reveal the shocking extent to which the controversial racial theory has infiltrated one of the most prestigious American service academies in the world. One presentation included in the set of documents teaches cadets that "racism is ordinary, race is socially constructed, and White Americans have primarily benefited from civil rights legislation. Everyone benefited from the civil rights laws.

The documents, which number over 600 pages, were released after the government watchdog group Judicial Watch sued the military twice under the Freedom of Information Act. The lawsuits were initiated after the Department of Defense failed to comply with a legally binding request for documents pertaining to cadet instruction. This training only further divides America.

Tom Fitton, president of Judicial Watch, was correct when he said, 'These documents show racist, anti-American CRT propaganda is being used to try to radicalize our rising generation of Army leadership at West Point.'

When you reflect on the national defense decisions of the White House and the Chairman of the Joint Chiefs of Staff, to include the Afghanistan withdrawal, mandatory vaccination for everyone in uniform, troop reduction, CRT training, and so many others that would take too long to list, it is easy to see that they are destroying our military, and quite candidly, I believe that is their goal. I am far from being alone when I say they should be removed from office and charged with treason.

And gentlemen, this is one of the major reasons, why America is becoming a Banana Republic. Thank you."

Steve added, "This is a suitable time for me to interject an item I had on my list.

According to a recent Gallop poll, 'Not only are Americans feeling grim about the current state of moral values in the nation, but they are also mostly pessimistic about the future on the subject, as 78 percent say morals are getting worse and just 18 percent say they are getting better. The latest percentage saying moral values are getting worse is roughly in line with the average of 74 percent since 2002, but it is well above the past two years' 67 percent and 68 percent readings.'

And evidence of that loss of moral values is everywhere you look. You can see it in the huge increase in our homicide rates, the increase in abortions, our sexual assault increases, and the hundreds of everyday larcenies that go unchecked. You can see it in our government with the everyday lies from our President down to many of our local mayors. You can see it in the two-tiered criminal system, the decisions of some prosecutors and judges. You can see it every time a federal or local law enforcement agency violates the Constitution or makes a phony arrest. You can see it in the riots with all the property destruction and this week we are seeing it in 'Jane's Revenge' in the group's fifty attacks on pregnancy centers.

No matter where you come from or what you believe or your political leaning, no one can deny that America and the quality of our life is declining rapidly,"

Jim concluded the State of America session by saying, "We have had many discussions on the challenges Putin has created by invading Ukraine. And to be honest, not one of us knows how it will end.

But China, which we have often discussed as well, is the one that keeps me awake at night. China's current trajectory poses significant challenges to nations around the world, including the United States. And right now, their military, their economic, and ideological ambitions are a global threat to the future of democracy and freedom. Their ultimate goal is to be the most powerful nation in the world and like Chuck, I believe they will invade Taiwan within the next few months and that scares the crap out of me. The President will do nothing since he and his son are in bed with Xi Jinping and in reality, America's foreign policy under this administration is meek, if not weak.

To sum it all up, the present state of America is not good. It is at its lowest level in its entire history. And that should scare the hell out of every American."

George told us, "Excuse me while I take this call on the case. I won't be long."

Jim told us to take a break and do whatever we need to do and we will pick it back up when George returns.

The call was longer than he expected, but George was ready to give us a case update. "This case is certainly unusual. Let me start by giving you the results of the canvass.

One woman who has a small window on the alley, heard a small explosion and saw a flash through the window. She confirmed it was exactly at 8:35 p.m. She cannot open the alley window, and she could not see the vehicle fire, but she did see a person wearing a 'dark baseball cap' walking in the alley away from the fire and she told me she thought he/she had a slight limp. She thought it was a man but was not sure. When asked, she said she never saw or heard any vehicles in the alley. Several other neighbors heard the explosion but saw nothing. When asked, all those interviewed stated that there is only an occasional vehicle in the alley.

There were no cameras on the alley side of all the buildings in this short block, which I find unusual these days. My best guess is that there was a reconnaissance of the area and the idiots chose this block because there were no cameras. I have to say this. Looks like they do their homework.

Presently there is a larger canvass in the area to see if we can find a person or a camera that put eyes on the Jeep or the person in the baseball cap or a vehicle waiting for him. That will take at least the rest of today because I told them I want an 8:35 p.m. surveillance and canvass also.

And now the interesting part. They could not restore the entire VIN because someone with the knowledge or someone who did their homework, took a welding torch to every other VIN location on the Jeep. And the lab stated, that given the rust, the torch work was done at least two years ago.

And now some rare, good news. The lab was able to restore part of the VIN digits and since they knew the year, make, and model they let the computer do the rest, which gave them eighty possible VIN's. Out of the eighty, only three were blue Jeeps. We are presently working to track down these three vehicles. Once we have the information, an FBI Agent from the nearest Field Office will be assigned to find that Jeep, get a statement from the owner and examine and photograph it for the report.

This may take a few days, but you will know five minutes after I do. Any questions?"

I knew someone was going to ask this and it was Joe.

"Do you know the significance of the numbers 8-3-5?" he asked with a smile.

George was quick to respond with a larger smile, "I certainly do. That was the time the shots were fired."

I always take good notes at my meetings and later review them making corrections and additions. It helps me refresh my memory if I end up testifying in a trial. That may be extremely optimistic on my part, but it has always worked for me and has saved some embarrassment along the way.

There was so much information from this morning's meeting, that I wanted to get my thoughts on paper as soon as possible. I had a quick, small lunch and went to my study where I sat at my desk for almost two hours adding notes and thoughts to what I had written during the meeting. Occasionally, I would pause and add a task to my "to do" list. This is not uncommon for those of us who have a mind that sometimes goes in a "hundred different directions." Okay, a hundred is an exaggeration, so let's try the number ten. In any case, you understand what I am trying to say.

When I finished, I called Tom Wilson and asked, "What records, in addition, to telephone numbers, does the FBI retain, that may help us find the significance of our 835 number. For example, I am sure the FBI could furnish us with a list of phone numbers with names, which contain the numbers 8-3-5, in that order. "

Tom replied, "I know they can create such a list, but I am quite sure they would not let us see it. Remember, despite a good working relationship with George, we are still the subjects of a criminal investigation. And secondly, if we did not do this covertly, and the rank and file got wind of it, the entire exercise would be a waste of time."

"I guess the same would go for the plate number on the Bureau cars," I said.

"Worse," Tom said. "FBI vehicle plate numbers are sacrosanct in the Bureau and are never let outside the Bureau. And if the Secret Service is anything like the Bureau, every agent has at least three different plates with accompanying registrations in their desk drawer."

"You're right," I said. "We did that also. Would it work if Judge Walters issued a subpoena for these files?"

"Probably not," Tom told me. "We know there is corruption in the upper echelon in the FBI, and I think we could already name a few that should be in prison. But we have no idea how far the corruption has spread. An hour after the subpoena hit the Hoover building, the paper shredders would be working overtime throughout the entire building and most likely in the Department of Justice building and the White House also. The reputations of the seven of us would be destroyed, our families would be humiliated, and WATCH24 would be out of business. Chuck, I have thought about this for weeks and I am as frustrated as you are. We have already been embarrassed by the integrity issues swarming around the FBI and Secret Services and I am mad as hell that these idiots are destroying the agencies, we dedicated our lives to.

I have prayed every day for some sort of Divine Intervention that would give us a path that finally ends this insanity and brings America back to the God-fearing country that made us all proud. But we do not know His timetable and we must patiently wait and hope it comes before it is too late."

"Tom, well-stated and I fully agree," I said. I have prayed every day also and there is power in prayer. But we both need to keep looking for answers and I trust our Lord will spread hints along our path."

Tom replied, "Looks like the three of us have a deal!"

"No free man shall ever be debarred the use of arms."
—Thomas Jefferson

CHAPTER 21

On Tuesday morning, at exactly 8:35 a.m., George sent a text message to the group:

"I am sure all of you noted the time of this message. Sorry, I couldn't help myself.

I have the information on the three blue Jeep Cherokees. The first one is registered to a man in Atlanta, Georgia. The second is owned by a company in Burlington, Vermont. I already sent a request to both FBI Field Offices to verify and photograph these vehicles. The third one, which I am assuming is the one we have, was crushed and sold for scrap metal in Tulsa, Oklahoma and the record states that the VIN plate was removed as required by law. What I do not understand, is the report does not list any previous owners. I called the FBI Lab supervisor I have been working with and asked him if there was any evidence that this Jeep was in a major accident. He stated, 'Absolutely not.' When

I told him the report did not list any previous owners, he told me that the only time he saw this was when it is purchased by the federal government for a 'classified operation,' and most of the time it is for the CIA.

We will dig further, and I will update you sometime this afternoon."

After my conversation with Tom yesterday afternoon, I was not going to look at this setback as a "brick wall," but as a "stone on the road."

As I was eating a late dinner, I was wondering why we never received an update from George. I did not have to wait long. Ten minutes later there was an emergency conference call from Jim. After he checked to make sure everyone was connected, he said, "Sorry if I interrupted your dinner, but George has an important update for us. Go ahead George."

George started, "I waited until I got home before I made this call. I am quite sure this is not the update that you were expecting because it was certainly not what I expected.

At 3:00 this afternoon, I received a call from the FBI Director's office telling me the Director wanted to see me in his office at 4:00 p.m. As I drove over to the FBI Hoover Building, I thought he just wanted to see how I was doing after the shooting. Instead, he wanted me to know that he was transferring me effective tomorrow to Headquarters and I would be working out of his office on a special project entitled, "Safety Procedures and Precautions for FBI agents." What a bunch of bullshit!

I will tell you what I think. It now appears to me that we may be getting too close to discovering how deep and wide the corruption is in the FBI, the Department of Justice and the Oval Office. He was never concerned about how I was doing, but he is sure as hell concerned about what we may discover. I know the look on my face told him I was not happy with this transfer, so figuring I had nothing to lose, I started asking questions:

'Who will be overseeing the shooting investigations?' He told me that it will stay in the Washington Field Office.

'Will I continue to receive updates?' That will be up to the Field Office, he stated.

And then I dropped the bombshell.

'Have you heard that the vehicle that engaged in both shootings has never been registered, most likely because it was purchased by the federal government for a classified investigation?' He replied, 'No, this type of information seldom gets to the Director's level.'

I told him that I had one request for him, 'Would you please have someone check to see if this Jeep was ever an FBI covert vehicle.'

'I am sure the Washington Field Office can manage that,' he said.

I could see he was becoming uncomfortable with the conversation. He told me to check with the desk on the way out to sign for my building pass, vehicle, and parking assignment."

Joe spoke up, "George, you and I are going to be busy for the next few days to make sure you are safe, and your words remain private."

George responded quickly, "I am one step ahead of you Joe. That is why I came home and am now sitting in a chair in my wife's large master bedroom closet with the door closed talking to all of you."

Everyone had a laugh and Joe replied, "Good for you. You are much more than one step ahead of me. For now, let's assume that they put a listening device or as we say a bug, in your house sometime after I installed the security system. I checked it that day and you were clean. Keep all conversations in the closet until I come to your home at exactly 1:10 a.m., tomorrow morning. At 1:00 a.m., turn off your security system and leave the back door unlocked. When I come in, do not speak to me until I speak to you. I will check the house again and install an additional device that will alert you by cell phone if anyone puts any type of spyware in or around your home. I will also give you a small device that I want you to place in your briefcase and take it with you to work tomorrow. When you get in your car in the morning, after a few minutes look at the device, if it is blinking red, do not talk. When you get settled in your new office, check to see if the device is green or red. When you get your new car, do the same thing. If there is a red light, text me when you get home, and I will take care of it. A GPS tracker on your car is not really a concern if you only drive from home to work and then back. If you need to go anywhere that would raise a red flag, we will have a WATCH24 agent pick you up. Remember your FBI car is in the parking garage eight hours every day unprotected, so frequent checks are mandatory. See you in the early morning and we will talk more."

Jim said, "Let's brainstorm for the next fifteen minutes or so and see what we can come up with. Does anyone have a good friend or contact that can be trusted in Tulsa?"

The General told us there is a retired Colonel that he has known for most of his adult life who is honest as the day is long. I would gladly call him, explain the situation, and see what he says.

I spoke up and asked George if there was a supervisor at the Washington Field Office that he fully trusted. George said there were two and he had already planned to see if they would help. I told him that he should call them on their home phones because someone is most likely reviewing phone records after we made them all paranoid.

Judge Walters spoke next, "This entire group has a high-level of credibility after the Sanchez case. There is a small group of federal judges that I know I can trust, since I play poker with them every month. If I whisper in their ears, they will call me if the FBI files any affidavits that are questionable or not routine.

Tom suggested that each of us know many retired and current agents. He thought that some of the more recent retired agents may have left because of the corruption and given the chance, any good cop wants the bad cops charged and purged.

Steve told us that the retired US Attorneys meet quarterly for lunch and the FBI corruption is always a topic of conversation. I will make sure that I am at the next luncheon which I believe is in three weeks.

Jim added, "The one tool that has worked for us is the digital meetings. George, we did have concerns about the agents that responded to the Mayflower Hotel. My understanding is that they were taking orders directly from the Department of Justice. It is time for another well-planned digital meeting?"

George replied, "That is true. There are two agents and an Assistant Agent-in-Charge assigned to a special investigation of our group that reports directly to DOJ. Obviously, we have committed no crimes. The sole purpose of this investigation is to keep this group from discovering their misdeeds and grand scheme.

As we ended the call, I was not sure if what took place today was a setback or the opportunity we were all hoping for. However, I am sure that it was in God's hands, and I find that comforting. My conversation with Tom on Monday had given me a surge of optimism. When I realized that I still felt optimistic, I partially recalled a saying that hung on my wall for fifty years:

Life's battles don't always go to
The Stronger or faster man;
But sooner or later the man who wins
Is the one who thinks he can.

A positive mental attitude can make all the difference in the world, and I must never forget that.

I reheated my dinner, ate a little more, cleaned the kitchen, and started the dishwasher. I looked at the clock and it was 8:35 p.m. How ironic, I thought. And just to be on the safe side, I said a prayer.

I got up early in the morning still filled with optimism and anxious to face today's challenges. I had a nice breakfast and decided to have my second cup of coffee in the den while I read the paper.

When I got to the third page of the paper, the reality of this unbelievable charade we are witnessing every day in our government destroyed my optimism. I could not believe what I was reading:

"The President's apparent senility was on full display last Thursday when, during a public meeting with several governors, he was seen holding a gigantic crib sheet containing childlike instructions on how to act."

Here are his instructions:

- YOU enter the Roosevelt Room and say hello.
- YOU take your seat.
- Press enters.
- YOU give brief comments.
- YOU ask President of AFL-CIO a question.
- YOU thank participants.
- YOU depart.

And this man is President of the United States and the alleged leader of the free world? I don't think so. It begs the question, "Who is really running American?" It certainly is not the Vice President. I thought to myself, if this does not scare the crap out of you, I do not know what would. This is insane and further proof that we are truly becoming a Banana Republic which put my mind in high speed. I tried to find an article that provided hope for America. I could not even find one. My frustration took over.

Every paper in the world will run this article and the result will be a decreasing respect for America which translates into a weaker America. Our enemies, Russia, Communist China, Iran and North Korea will take advantage of our weakness to increase their own power, and unfortunately, the world we once knew, may never appear again.

We have never seen America so divided, which precludes the use of Article 25 of the Constitution to remove the President. There is a point where the declination of America could lead to total chaos or even civil war.

There was one more article in the paper that epitomizes the

decline in law and order, which is the most important ingredient for a healthy, safe America. A summarized version follows:

A 34-year-old "professional" NYC shoplifter is the new poster child for the failure of bail reform in this state. After his latest arrest this week—his 50th this year—for petit larceny for shoplifting and criminal possession of a controlled substance, he was released on his own recognizance. He is no stranger to the legal system as he has two felonies and twenty-nine misdemeanor convictions to his credit as well as 20 missed court appearances.

Incredibly, before this latest arrest and despite the number of arrests this year alone, he does not have any open cases currently against him. The Manhattan District Attorney was quoted as saying, "We cannot accept a system where individuals who shoplift repeatedly cycle in and out of jail, just to shoplift again."

Liberal Prosecutors throughout our country are disregarding established laws and guidelines and releasing violent felons to commit more violent acts.

The man who shot and killed two El Monte Police Officers, Michael Paredes and Joseph Santana, as they responded to a domestic violence call, was already on probation for illegal possession of firearms. He had been sentenced to three years but received a lenient plea deal in line with Los Angeles County District Attorney.

All we want from our prosecutors is for them to follow their oath of office and do their jobs. Removing the revolving doors from their office, and prosecuting violent felons without reducing the original charges, would be a good start.

We desperately need to try our best to eliminate the insanity and repair our country, but we cannot do it without God's help.

And I am going to do my best to remain optimistic.

"No police department can remain free of corruption in a community where bribery flourishes in public office and private enterprise; a corrupt police department in an otherwise corruption-free society is a contradiction in terms."
—O. W. Wilson

CHAPTER 22

I knew the Thursday morning Zoom meeting was going to be mostly dedicated to the shooting investigation, so I emailed the two newspaper articles to our group to save time.

I decided today to brainstorm and try to find the holes in the armor of those who are attempting to change America to a social Banana Republic.

We all know that the Federal Bureau of Investigation is not totally corrupt. But what I can't understand are the agents and supervisors who receive an order or assignment from their boss and comply knowing they are breaking the law, ignoring the Constitution and/or violating their oath of office. How do they put their heads on a pillow and sleep at night? Is the climate inside the FBI so toxic and threatening that everyone is in fear of losing their job? Do they think just because someone else lied to a judge and a search warrant has been issued that they are exempt from their internal rules and their sworn oath of office? Do they think if the order came from the Director, the Department of Justice or the Oval Office, they could not question it? Or are they just so full of themselves that they are convinced they are above the law because they are the "good guys" and the end justifies the means?

I do not know the answers to these questions. But what I do know is that most of them would jump at the chance to help return honesty and integrity to the FBI if their identity could be protected. That puts hundreds of holes in the armor of the FBI. The problem is that if we reach through the hole and get the wrong person, everything could blow up. This is one of those tasks that requires you to do your homework.

It is much more complicated in the Department of Justice since the Department is inherently political and full of lawyers. Unless we can find a DOJ lawyer with a history of high ethical behavior, who is willing to tell us everything, put his lawyer friends in jail, have his family threatened, and does not mind being thrown into the middle of a media circus, we are better off looking elsewhere.

Millions of dollars and guaranteed total immunity would poke a hole in the White House armor, but we can't go there or we wouldn't be able to sleep at night.

Let's go back to the 8-3-5 dilemma. After much thought, I am going to place all my chips on telephone numbers. I think we should look at what we do know, and disregard, for the time being, that which we do not know.

I do not believe that the shooting of Mark was unintentional. They were definitely sending us a message.

George and Mark were the only agents in the Washington Field Office that were helping us. And the circumstances that led up to us getting help from them, were vastly different.

Obviously, they torched the Jeep someplace where it would be discovered immediately. They could have driven it twenty miles away and found a dirt road in the woods. And unless it started a huge forest fire, we probably would not have known for weeks or more. They wanted us to take possession of that vehicle.

When you add all this up, you start looking for a scenario where this would make sense. I am going out on the limb with this one. But I think the person who was driving the Jeep is somehow on our side. I do not think he is an undercover cop, but he may have a history as a paid informant. And he is covertly sending us clues to break this case. He is not a psychopath or a sociopath who enjoys playing mind games with the police. He is intentionally trying to help us. And that is why I think the 8:35 p.m. time must be related to something simple and in our view every day And I think is related to a single telephone number.

I did not want to wait until Thursday to share my thoughts, so I sent a text message to everyone. I knew that George did not feel comfortable using his WATCH24 cell phone at work, especially on the first day. So, I asked Joe to tell him if they spoke in the late afternoon.

Tom Wilson called me immediately and told me he thought I may be right.

Jim called and said, "Chuck, unless something else credible comes up, that is the direction we are going to take."

By mid-afternoon, I was worn out and decided to take a nap. When my cell phone woke me up, I glanced at my watch and was surprised that it was almost 5:00 p.m. It was Joe with a text message:

"Good afternoon. This is an update on the trials and tribulations of George. First the good news. His home and his past FBI vehicle were clear—no bugs. His office has a listening device which I believe is a wireless FM transmitter going to a digital recorder within two hundred feet. Now that we know, George is going to be on his best behavior and be careful with visitors who may try to entrap him into something he would not normally say. He won't have any trouble with this.

His phone is being monitored also, so no calls to his office and his WATCH24 cell will be locked in his home safe in the 'off' position when he is at work.

George will be on his way home from work in his new FBI vehicle and he needs to stop at the grocery store to buy milk or beer, his choice. Once he is in the store, I will park next to his car and walk to the trunk of his car and then up close on the passenger's side door. The equipment in my car will do the rest of the work. I will go into the store and my choice will be beer. Once I leave and drive away, George will come out of the store and go home.

Thirty minutes after I get home, I will send a text and update everyone."

I must admit, Joe is extremely witty and his sense of humor can put a smile on your face, no matter what the circumstances. I also think Joe has figured it out that we expect to hear some humor from him, or we would be disappointed. He is right and he never lets us down.

It was 7:25 p.m. when we received the text from Joe:

"Just as I thought, George's FBI vehicle has a listening device probably with a hidden digital recorder that can be downloaded without being removed. It also has a GPS tracking device that goes to a computer in the Hoover Building and shows the exact location 24/7. We may want to use that to our advantage someday.

I have documented all of this, and I have it in sealed evidence envelop. Tom, I will deliver it to you tomorrow and get your signature.

Remember the spy's golden rule: Bugging without a court order is a crime; debugging is not."

On Wednesday morning, we all received a text message from Jim: *"Before George went to work this morning, he called to tell me that since his new position does not give him the same flexibility he had in his former position, he would be unable to participate in the Zoom meetings. I told him we cannot allow that. I asked him if he would be able to make the meetings if I changed the time to 5:00 a.m. to 7:00 a.m. That will work for him. So, get to bed early tonight, grab an early cup of coffee, and I will see all your smiling faces on my computer screen at 5:00 a.m.*

Yawning is allowed."

In the afternoon, Ben set up another call with Kim, Marie and Katherine. It was an enjoyable conversation with many questions and answers going back and forth. Marie told me Jason is doing good and every other night after work, he and Bob, the

WATCH24 Agent, go out to dinner. I know that all is going fine with everyone, because no one asked when they could come home, and that's okay. We are not out of the woods yet.

Trust me, there was noticeable yawning at the Thursday early morning Zoom meeting. Any time you upset a senior's daily schedule, there will be fallout. I am just hoping we complete the meeting before someone's head is resting on the laptop keyboard.

Jim opened by thanking everyone for getting up so early and George told us how much he appreciated the change in time so he could participate. He also asked if we could skip the Monday morning Zoom meeting and use a conference call if needed. We all agreed. I think Jim is easing us into the new schedule.

Steve started the conversation on the shooting investigation by asking, "Do we know anything more on our blue Jeep?"

George replied, "As you know, I am no longer a part of the investigation and even though I am one of the victims, my best guess is that the only words I will hear are, 'we are working on it.' I doubt that anyone is following up on the blue Jeep."

Jim suggested, "Let's pause here until we resolve this problem. Does anyone know an FBI Agent who was in the Tulsa Field Office from 2015 to today?"

Tom Wilson spoke up," Years ago I worked in the Chicago Field Office as a Supervisor, and Henry Parsons who was from Tulsa was in my unit. Since we were both single at the time, we shared a small flat. I am not sure where he is now, but I trust him and will look him up and see if he can help."

Jim reminded us, "We have a small WATCH24 office in Tulsa if you need any help.

Chuck sent all of us a text on his theory on the case. Does

anyone have a comment or question for him?

George said, "Monday, I took all my personal files home after being told I was being transferred. If your experiences are like mine, half the people you arrest tell you that they are a police informant, which could be true in Washington DC, which has the highest per capita ratio of informants in the world. It was so frequent and so difficult to verify, I started collecting names for my own file, so the agents did not have to start from ground zero each time we encountered a 'police informant.' I will review it this evening and let you know if I find anything."

Judge Walters added, "The entire world is aware how political and corrupt the FBI has become. If we allow their corruption to stall our investigation, the bad guys win. Let's keep pushing, and when, these small obstacles grow to a huge brick wall, put every credible piece of information in an affidavit, and I will flood them with subpoenas. This will send them into a panic, hopefully produce some honest whistleblowers, and give us another chance."

General Monroe stated, "Judge Walters is correct. From a military perspective, this is no longer a battle, it is a full-blown war that will destroy America unless we win. And if you want further proof, listen carefully.

In an article written by the Center for Preventive Action, titled, A cyberattack on the US Power Grid, in part, states the following:

> 'The US power grid has long been considered a logical target for a major cyberattack. Besides the intrinsic importance of the power grid to a functioning US society, all sixteen sectors of the US economy deemed to make up the nation's critical infrastructure rely on electricity. Disabling or otherwise

interfering with the power grid in a significant way could thus seriously harm the United States.

Carrying out a cyberattack that successfully disrupts grid operations would be extremely difficult, but not impossible. Such an attack would require months of planning, significant resources, and a team with a broad range of expertise. Although cyberattacks by terrorist and criminal organizations cannot be ruled out, the capabilities necessary to mount a major operation against the US power grid make potential state adversaries the principal threat.

Short of outright conflict with a state adversary, several plausible scenarios in which the US power grid would be subject to cyberattack need to be considered:

- *Discrediting Operations.* Given the importance of electricity to the daily lives of Americans, an adversary may see advantage in disrupting service to undermine public support for a US administration at a politically sensitive time.

- *Distracting Operations.* A state contemplating a diplomatic or military initiative likely to be opposed by the United States, could carry out a cyberattack against the US power grid that would distract the attention of the US government and disrupt or delay its response.

- *Retaliatory Operations.* In response to US actions considered threatening by another state, such as the imposition of economic sanctions and various forms of political warfare, a cyberattack on the power grid could be carried out to punish the United States or intimidate it from taking further action with the implied threat of further damage.

There are many plausible circumstances in which states that possess the capability to conduct cyberattacks on the US power grid-principally Russia and China, and potentially Iran and North Korea-could contemplate such action for the reasons elaborated above.

However, considerable potential exists to miscalculate both the impact of a cyberattack on the US grid and how the US government might respond. Attacks could easily inflict much greater damage than intended, in good part because the many health and safety systems that depend on electricity could fail as well, resulting in widespread injuries and fatalities. Given the fragility of many industrial control systems, even reconnaissance activity risks accidentally causing harm. An adversary could also underestimate the ability of the United States to attribute the source of a cyberattack, with important implications for what happens thereafter. Thus, an adversary's expectations that it could attack the power grid anonymously and with impunity could be unfounded."

General Monroe continued, "The intelligence community agrees with us and clearly states that the weakness of our current Administration increases the likelihood the United States of America will experience a cyberattack against our power grid before the end of the year.

A large-scale cyberattack on the power grid could inflict considerable damage. For example, the 2003 Northeast Blackout left fifty million people without power for four days and caused economic losses between $4 billion and $10 billion, according to the Center for Preventive Action.

Our politicians have given a lot of lip service to cyberattacks, but very few preventive actions have occurred. We are much more vulnerable than the federal government admits, and the results will be measured in more than economics, they will also be measured by body count."

General Monroe concluded, "A weak and inept President and a weak Attorney General lead to corruption, an enormous increase in crime and a two-tiered justice system. And that same weak President with an inept Department of Defense, and a weakened military, led to a failed withdrawal from Afghanistan, over seven billion dollars of arms and equipment left to the enemy, possibly Armageddon."

And on that sobering note, the Thursday Zoom meeting ended and trust me, no one fell asleep.

It is now 8:00 in the morning and I am already exhausted. I am not sure if it is because of the lack of sleep, the intensity of the Zoom meeting, my age, or a combination of all three. In any case, I need a break from all of it and vowed to put everything on hold until Monday. I have more than enough other projects to keep me occupied for three days.

"Tolerance will reach such a level that the intelligent people will be banned from thinking so as to not offend the imbeciles."
—Dostoevsky

CHAPTER 23

As I had hoped, the weekend was quiet, and I really enjoyed eliminating more than half of my "to-do" list. The yard and the garage, the only room I have total control of which I am certain is true for most men, are looking much better. Too bad Kim wasn't here to see them.

So today, with renewed vigor, I am going to jump back into the case and prepare for Thursday's 5:00 a.m. Zoom meeting.

Just as I was sitting down at my desk, we all received a group conference call from Tom Wilson.

Tom began, "Over the weekend, I located Henry Parson's home phone number and gave him a call. There was no answer, but I did leave a voice mail for him to give me a call ASAP.

He called back this morning and apologized for not getting back to me sooner, but he and his wife were away for the weekend.

The first thing he said was, 'Tom, even though I am going to retire from the Bureau at the end of the year, if you are calling me to tell me they finally fired all those corrupt asses in the Puzzle Palace (Hoover Building) and you are going to be the Director again, I may want to stay a few more years.'

I did have to laugh. I told Henry, which is not going to happen and I am not sure I would take it if they did offer it. But I need a favor. I then asked if he could check a vehicle for me.

When I mentioned the 2015 dark blue Jeep Cherokee, his response surprised me, "I don't need to check on it, I could write a book about it. That vehicle was in this office and assigned to the Joint Terrorism Task Force. Why do you ask?"

I explained that we had picked up that vehicle on surveillance cameras as the one doing covert surveillance on our homes and involved in two shooting incidents at FBI Agent's homes.

Henry said that is impossible. He told me their vehicle was accidentally crushed for salvage and an agent got disciplined for the mistake. He was shocked when I told him the FBI laboratory had the vehicle as evidence stored in a garage.

I gave him all the details and he said, 'I will tell you who you need to talk to, Agent Jim Duffy, and I do not know if he is still in the Bureau.' Henry told me the rumor in the Tulsa Office was that Duffy had a Godfather, not sure if it was literally or figuratively, in high places in the Justice Department and that is why he only got a mild reprimand for the Jeep incident.

I told Henry that it would be premature to question Duffy at this time, and our conversation needed to stay confidential. He agreed. Steve, I told him that you would contact him on his home phone and get whatever you need from him. I will text you his number as soon as the call ends.

I am not sure where this is heading but we need to be extremely cautious. I am not sure if this was luck, or good police work, or Divine Intervention, but it gave us a different path to follow. We need to tread lightly."

"I think it was a combination of the three," Judge Walters added.

When the call ended, I said a prayer of thanks and praise. God's hands were present for this one.

I also made myself a note to call George at home tonight to keep him current. I believe Duffy was one of the agents that responded to the first digital meeting at the Mayflower. It will be interesting to hear George's comments on this.

It now appears that the Thursday morning Zoom meeting may be the one that gets us heading in the right direction. And Tom was right, we must be cautious. In this case, there is no conventional way to send a subpoena to the FBI and expect compliance. They will ignore it, go into a full-blown cover-up mode, destroy evidence, make no comment and hire lawyers. We have seen this scenario in the federal government many times before.

I sat at my desk for several hours and wrote truly little. It is difficult to create a "sting operation" without an undercover operative on the inside. I know that most of the agents are honest and would offer to testify, but currently we cannot distinguish the good from the bad. We risk everything if we approach them, so we have no other choice but to wait for them to come forward. And if they do, they put their careers, their family, and quite possibly their lives at risk. Not a good situation.

I had an early dinner from my frozen dinner stock and realized I only had eight remaining. Looks like I will need to do some meal planning in addition to my Zoom meeting planning. I miss Kim.

At 7:00 p.m., I called George and using my notes, I attempted to accurately repeat Tom's call from this morning.

His first comment was, "That is very interesting for many reasons."

I then asked, "Do you know if Jim Duffy was one of the agents that responded to the Mayflower Hotel when we had our first digital meeting?"

George replied, "But I can't be sure. As you know, Duffy was on a special assignment working for the Justice Department and we had no control of him. Any reports were submitted to whoever he was working for in Justice. We did not like the situation but had to tolerate it. We also had heard that Duffy had a relative or Godfather in the Justice Department, but never heard a name. Duffy was cocky and somewhat a cowboy. In other words, he was his supervisor's nightmare and that is why they did not mind that he was on special assignment."

I told George that this will be discussed at the Thursday morning Zoom meeting.

George said, "Good. You gave me a lot to digest. I need to think about it, but I will be ready on Thursday morning. Thanks for the call."

I remembered that Watch24 has photos of the two agents that were at the Mayflower. I will make sure the photos are available on Thursday morning so we can verify their names.

I would also like an update on the FBI's investigation of the dirty bombs.

On Tuesday morning at 11:00 a.m., I received a text message from Ben at the safe house telling me that Kim would be calling me from his phone in ten minutes and not to worry, everything is fine. Ben knows me well and did not leave me hanging. That is why he included those last three words.

Kim seemed excited to talk to me. After we made sure each of us were okay, but miss being together, Kim said, " I have got some good news for a change."

I immediately thought that she was going to tell me that Sharon was expecting. I was wrong.

"Joe was here yesterday afternoon and he stopped by to say hello and check to see if I needed anything," Kim told me.

I replied, "That's Joe. He is a devoted friend."

Kim continued, "It gets better. I told Joe that we would love it if he stayed and had dinner with us. He thanked me but said maybe the next time. He told me he needed to head home after he installs a piece of new equipment in the lodge.

During the installation of the equipment, Joe met Ann Smith and suddenly he had time for dinner with us. From a woman's perspective, it seems to me that they enjoyed each other's company. And after dinner, Joe and Ann sat in the living room and talked for another hour. Poor guy must have really been tired when he got home. Now isn't that good news."

"Yes, it is good news," I said. "Joe has been divorced for close to eleven years and I would hate to think that he would be alone for the remainder of his life.

"And don't you tell anyone." Kim concluded. Let's see how it goes. And since everyone here is aware of it, it will get out soon enough."

After talking to Kim, I thought what good news this really was. Joe is such a kind, gentle man, he deserves a life of happiness.

In preparing for Thursday's Zoom meeting, I discovered a report from The Intercept, entitled, The Left-Wing City Just Brought China's Surveillance to America. The report reads in part:

"Washington, DC is the ultimate haven for big government. They are the home to the worst authoritarian politicians and Deep State officials who want nothing more than to control the American public.

This was clearly shown last year when they decided to expand the Capitol Police to become a national surveillance agency like the FBI.

Now they are stepping up their surveillance against their own citizens even further, and it is getting ugly.

The Metropolitan Police Department (MPD) has created a special surveillance unit called the Joint Operations Command Center (JOCC) which watches the citizens of DC, day and night.

The MPD designed the JOCC as a surveillance control center. It contains more than 20 display monitors linked to around 50 computer stations, all connected to the MPD's broad arsenal of intelligence data programs and surveillance sources."

This surveillance apparatus has been getting worse and worse for years, and only now is it finally being brought to light in the public eye.

For years, this sprawling web of surveillance has been shrouded in secrecy. Now, more than two decades into the frenzy of police monitoring of ordinary citizens, recently uncovered documents are revealing its scope and practices."

It is amazing to think that a government could have such an extensive program to target its own citizens without anyone on the outside even knowing about it.

The mayor of DC and her cohorts went to extreme lengths to keep this program hidden from public view, because they knew there would be outrage if it was ever discovered.

The article continues, "Until 2021, the Council of Governments operated a secret face-recognition tech system, data from which it shared with 14 local and federal agencies.

This information-sharing is incredibly dangerous because it means that federal agencies just keep growing and growing their databases of American citizens.

When local police departments share their surveillance information with federal Deep State agencies, they just empower those agencies to target even more American citizens like they are doing now."

This Administration's domestic war on terror is targeted at conservatives. They used the FBI to target parents who were protesting Critical Race Theory, while the American borders remain unprotected, crime is out of control, gas is over five dollars a gallon, food prices have increased by eighteen percent and the middle class is struggling to survive. But these are not priorities. Their top priority is to prevent the law-abiding conservative citizens from returning the power to the people and saving America from socialism. It cuts me to the core knowing our world has turned upside down.

With everyone present, the Thursday morning Zoom meeting began at 4:45 a.m., proving there is still enthusiasm in the senior population.

Jim started the meeting by putting eight photos on the screen. He then asked if anyone could tell him the names of the two men in the photographs on their screen.

Without hesitation, George stated, "The top four pictures are Agent Jim Duffy and the bottom four are Agent Rick Barber. And to be more exact it is 'James' and 'Richard.'"

Jim said, "Thank you . Those are the names we had and just wanted verification."

George spoke next, "I wanted to take the time to explain how I am addressing my new position in FBI Headquarters. As you recall my assignment is to produce a report titled "Safety Procedures and Precautions for FBI agents."   That is broad enough for me to go in any number of ways. I am determined to do a thorough report and submitted an outline to the Director with a list of what I would like to review for the report. The list includes on and off duty deaths of agents, on duty injuries of agents that resulted in disability retirements, on duty injuries that required more than ten days of hospitalization, off duty injuries or illnesses resulting in sick leave of over thirty days and any cases of Post-Traumatic Stress Disorder resulting in more than thirty days sick leave.

I made an appointment with the Director to discuss this with him. Fortunately for us, after he reviewed it, his phone rang, and he started to hand it back to me. I asked him to please initial it and he did and pointed to the door for me to leave. Obviously, he did not want me in the room during the conversation.

And now I have written approval by the Director to access personnel files.

After Chuck and I talked on Monday evening, I knew we needed to review Duffy's file to include his background investigation to see if we could identify his 'Godfather.' However, if we needed to use any of this information in court, we could run into a problem. Judge Walters and Steve may want to comment."

Steve went first. "My general rule is always file an affidavit with the court and request a subpoena and then you do not have to worry about it." The Judge agreed with Steve.

Chuck added, "But then we have the problem of serving the subpoena on the FBI. They will ignore it, begin the cover-up and hire attorneys. And we will be no further ahead."

After he let that sink in, George spoke again, "I never like to state a problem without offering a solution. Listen carefully and see if this works. I am now working in the Director's Office. Is there anything that prevents me from accepting subpoenas? I would log in the subpoena and provide the requested records. I believe that only subpoenas requesting arrest information and investigative reports go to FBI attorneys for review. Routine personnel file requests were so numerous they no longer review them unless something unusual is brought to their attention. I really do not see anything unusual here."

Jim stated, "Unless anyone sees it differently, I think we have resolved one of our major problems thanks to George."

Tom changed the subject by telling us, "I have been asked to update the group on the two dirty bombs. For two weeks now I have been asking the El Paso Field Office for an update. Evidently, the bosses were told to ignore my calls. I called yesterday and asked to speak to any supervisor and ended up with one of the Assistant Special Agents. He was much more respectful and in confidence, told me, 'Director, I honestly no longer know what is going on with the Bureau, but that case has been pulled from us and allegedly sent to a special unit for investigation. We have not heard a word about the case. Most of us think the special unit was the paper shredder. Please do not quote me on this.'"

Shaking his head in disbelief, Tom continued, "I cannot put in words how heart broken and disgusted I am with the FBI. I never thought I would say this, but the present structure of the Bureau that allows the corruption we are witnessing, needs to be eliminated."

And not surprisingly, no one disagreed with him.

Chuck added one more thought before the meeting ended. "I still believe that the driver of the Jeep is attempting to help us. Keep looking for that 8-3-5."

As soon as the meeting ended, Jim called me. "Chuck, did you talk to Kim yesterday?"

I had to play along and said, "Yes, why do you ask?"

"Are you telling me she did not tell you about Joe and Ann?" he asked.

I started laughing and I said, "I am kidding with you. They are both wonderful people and I will pray that it works out for them."

"The only effective way to ensure the value of the future is to confront the present courageously and constructively."
    —Rollo May

CHAPTER 24

The case has made some amazing progress this week, but we are missing something. The fact that the FBI has no active investigation on the two dirty bombs troubles me. And what was accomplished by firing shots into two agents' homes? What was the reason for casing two of our homes? Do the strange actions of the Washington Field Office have anything to do with the Mexican drug cartels? There are so many questions and so few answers.

But the most important, looming question is, "What is the ultimate end game this Administration is hoping to accomplish." Obviously, one aspect is their quest for power and money, but if America becomes a Banana Republic, what is truly gained?

The President and his administration are violating the law daily by sending a clear message throughout the world that anyone who wants to get into America is welcome and the door is open. And they will be treated better than American citizens. Illegal aliens are given free healthcare, free cell phones, and free baby formula at the border. They will do whatever they can to give illegal aliens the right to vote and citizenship through a massive amnesty scheme.

This is a deliberate effort to "fundamentally transform" America and the White House is openly proud of it. However, there is a terrible cost to the President's illegal policies.

The recent deaths of 53 migrants in San Antonio are the direct result of these policies.

Thousands of young Americans are dying from a record number of drug overdoses driven by fentanyl coming from Communist China and Mexico through the open borders.

The Border Patrol agents apprehended 15 people listed on the FBI's terror watch list sneaking across the US-Mexico border in May, bringing the total since last October to 50. It is unfortunate that our federal government has no idea how many crossed successfully and are presently living in our communities.

Crime is rising throughout the country at alarming rates with little hope of a recovery.

The Constitution and laws are being ignored by many of our elected officials and federal law enforcement. Their oath of office is also ignored and no longer serves any useful purpose.

Free speech in under attack daily.

The main street media no longer serves as the fourth leg of democracy.

Under the last administration, the United States became energy independent. In his first few weeks in office, the President closed the Keystone XL pipeline eliminating 11,000 jobs.

Inflation in America is now over 8 percent and expected to

go higher. Gasoline is over five dollars a gallon. Food prices are almost 18 percent higher under the current administration and food shortages are rising.

Mortgage rates are rising, and insurance costs are increasing dramatically.

Middle class Americans are living paycheck to paycheck while their credit card debt is increasing each month.

When you examine all this collectively, any intelligent person would conclude that this President's and Administration's ultimate end game is the destruction of America. I believe this to be true. I just do not understand what they hope to gain. But know this. Going unchecked, these domestic enemies will destroy America much faster than any of our foreign enemies.

There is another way to view all of this. Robert W. Malone MD, MS, explains it this way in his article, "Who is Robert Malone."

> *"I have written extensively on* inverted totalitarianism*, that being the once nascent, now entrenched form of government that truly controls the levers of federal power in the United States. This behemoth has turned the USA into a "managed democracy;" a bureaucracy which cannot be held accountable by the elected representatives of the people. Sometimes called the Fourth Estate, this monster is also referred to as the "deep state" the civil service, or the administrative state.*
>
> *Inverted totalitarianism does not have an authoritarian leader, but instead is run by a non-transparent group of bureaucrats. This unelected, invisible ruling class runs the country from within. They are easily influenced by corporate interests due to both the lure of powerful jobs after federal employment and*

the capture of our legislative bodies by the lobbyists serving concealed corporate interests."

Doctor Malone's definition of the "deep state," clearly defines a large part of the problem, but right now I am at a loss to suggest any solution. For years, we have been talking about term limits for members of Congress which would necessitate a change in the Constitution. It appears to me that placing limits on federal government employees would be much easier. However, that would also mean that it would be just as easy to revert to no limits. I am certain that the Convention of States could help America find a solution. Americans need to support this group."

On Friday evening, we received a group text message from George:

"Today I asked for specific agent personnel files for my project. I am allowed to review up to five at a time and must return them the following day, except any files I have on Friday, must be returned before the end of the day. Makes sense. All medical files will be reviewed by the Bureau physician to comply with the Health Insurance Portability and Accountability Act or HIPPA, which is great as far as I am concerned. I met him today and I do not think I will have a problem collaborating with him, but I will be cautious.

I tell you all of this because I know we are all anxious to see Duffy's file, but I need to ease myself into the process. Today, all the files were agents who were killed in the line of duty. I met Linda who will be helping me. And we both signed a form that has the time and date that I received the file. I am not sure, but this is probably the same process for taking a file to respond to a subpoena. Be patient. I will figure a way to secretly get the information we need.

Have a good weekend."

George is such a detail person; he is definitely the man for the task. I have confidence that he will eventually get the information we need. The sooner, the better.

The weekend remained quiet and gave me time to prepare for the Monday morning Zoom meeting, which I completed on Saturday. Sunday was reserved for church and Tom and Sharon invited me over to their place for dinner at 3:00 p.m. Perhaps they will have some news for Grandpa!

"Our national politics has become a competition for images or between images, rather than between ideals."
—Daniel J. Boorstin

CHAPTER 25

The Monday morning Zoom meeting started right on time, unlike last week when we were fifteen minutes early.

General Monroe started the meeting. "I understand that the Governor of Virginia urged the Pentagon to drop its vaccine mandate for Army National Guard Troops ahead of a June 30 deadline. In a letter obtained by The Daily Caller News Foundation, the Governor and several Republican Virginia representatives argued that the vaccine mandate would harm the Guard's ability to accomplish its duties. It was reported that up to 40,000 National Guardsmen and 20,000 reservists who have rejected the COVID-19 vaccine face discharge.

NBC News is reporting that military recruitment in 2022 has plummeted, leaving the Pentagon scrambling for ways to fill the ranks of US forces. Alienation of traditional families, who constitute the military's core recruiting market, through things like diversity quotas, refusing religious exemptions and teaching Critical Race Theory at military institutions have all contributed to a growing unwillingness to enlist. The result is a loss of prestige and meritocracy in the armed forces, according to the Center for Military Readiness.

The culture of the military has been eroded by several years of social engineering and woke policies. And it has been accelerated by the current administration."

After a short pause, General Monroe continued, "After all my years in the Army, I never thought I would see this day. In addition, the Army has announced a plan to temporarily reduce the size of the active-duty force, from 485,000 soldiers down to 473,000 by 2023, for 'quality' considerations, whatever the hell that means. I will tell you what it means, a weak and under strength military leads to a weak nation which jeopardizes the safety of America and the world. And I find that sickening."

Judge Walters added, "So let me see if I can get my arms around all of this. Crime is rising and out of control, there is very little law and order, police recruiting across the country is worse than the military, inflation is above eight percent, gasoline is over five dollars a gallon, food supplies are decreasing, we are no longer energy independent, the younger generation is waiting for more handouts from the government rather than looking for jobs, thousands of people are illegally entering our country every month, Russia is at war with Ukraine, Communist China is preparing to invade Taiwan, North Korea is testing ballistic missiles, Iran is rapidly growing stockpiles of enriched uranium to 60 percent purity, a short, technical step away from weapons-grade levels, this administration wants to take away our guns, and we have a President, in name only, who apparently does not give a damn about the American people or the country. This is insanity. Governments have been overthrown for much less.

This has been going on since the day this President took his oath of office, which evidently meant nothing to him. Every time we get an update, we see our country sinking into a deeper hole. We cannot continue down this road and exist as a free nation and it is going to take a lot more than the seven of us to turn it around.

We need to move ahead and be ready for what lies ahead. As soon as the corruption starts to be exposed, we must control the narrative in the country and not allow the left and the main street media spread their lies. If we can do that, I trust that silent majority, all the good, honest citizens from every generation, will spring to our side and we will have a force, that will be much larger than you can imagine. It will be a celebration unlike anyone has ever seen in our entire history.

I thought this could wait a while longer on this, but the way things are moving, let me list our priorities:

Manpower

Each of us will work in our areas of expertise and find the highest-level supervisors you can trust. Then let them fill their team with ones they trust. The more teams we have the more we can accomplish and the faster we can return the government to the people. You can start working on it now. I already have a list of twenty judges that we will be able to use on day one. I just haven't told them yet.

Search Warrants

Start making lists of all the search warrants you will need, starting with the shooter all the way up to the White House.

We can hopefully fill in the names as the investigation progresses.

Always seize laptops and cell phones ASAP. This disrupts their line of communication and prevents them from warning any cohorts. Remember when no one answers, seventy percent leave a message which can be great evidence. Track down any evidence that will help our case, i.e., calendars, day timers, phone records, correspondence, files, bank statements. Ask to search their desk. If they refuse, get a search warrant if necessary. The majority of people place the items they care most about in their right drawers.

Remember seizure can include possession by control as long as it is secured. As an example, you could seize the Department of Justice file room, if it is properly secured. If necessary, you could use armed guards 24/7 if that is what it takes to prevent evidence tampering and proof of continuity of evidence. You must be able to show that no unauthorized person was allowed to penetrate your security perimeter. But always remember, desperate people do desperate things and we still do not know all our enemies, to include those in the deep state.

Indictments

We will have a single grand jury for our initial indictments. Obviously, we won't be able to indict everyone that has committed a crime, before it breaks wide open, but file all the charges and Steve and Tony Lopez will seek indictments for the leaders and main players which hopefully creates chaos in their structure.

Once everyone in the world knows about the investigation, we will have up to three grand juries running simultaneously. Steve has already completed his list of six additional prosecutors to keep things moving. The day a person is indicted, if possible, will be the day that person is arrested. If possible, we will try not to arrest anyone when young children are present.

Public Relations

This is the one task needed to keep the entire process free of catastrophic problems. Anytime there is an incident or event, the left will put a spin on it that benefits their side and their agenda and attempts to make the other side, concerned honest citizens, law enforcement, judges, conservative mothers, Christians, Jews, etc., look like 'deplorables,' criminals or extremists. Just look at the Supreme Court decisions, the January 6th demonstration, or the associated trials for examples.

Many of these planned chaotic events can be prevented with early messages that explain the action as being necessary in the interest of safety along with a no tolerance policy on criminal behavior.

Media Releases

Jim and I have each chosen two media professionals (Bill Rounds and Janice Buckley) who will start working with us this week and will help us get our message out when we are ignored by the main street media. Each of you will be visited by Bill and Janice sometime this week so you can get to know them and use them when needed. However, given all the experience in this room, you may answer any questions you get from the media, just let Janice or Bill know about it.

All the information I just gave you will be included in small pocket handbook that will be given to every person that works on this investigation to include all WATCH24 staff. An alphabetic phone directory will also be in the handbook."

Jim stated, "I know this has been a lengthy presentation this morning, but we all needed to hear this. Thank you. We have about fifteen minutes left. The floor is open."

Steve let us know that the grand jury panel has all been screened and will be sworn in the first day they are called into session and that Toney Lopez is now working on the investigation every day.

I spoke up, "The Judge is right. Time is not on our side. We need to carefully start pushing buttons that will expose the corruption and advance our case. I just want everyone to think about it and we can discuss it at Thursday's Zoom meeting."

Joe then made an offer to the group, "I need to go to the safe house this week, if anyone wants to visit their family."

George jumped at the chance and said, "Joe, I would like to go with you and surprise my wife. Is Saturday okay for you?"

Joe replied, "Works for me."

And neither Jim nor I said a word.

"As I grow older, I pay less attention to what men say, I just watch what they do."
—Andrew Carnegie

CHAPTER 26

On Wednesday evening at 8:05 p.m., George sent a text message to all of us.

"This morning I got an envelope from the Washington Field Office requesting my signature on several agent evaluations. Unfortunately, Agent Duffy was not on the list.

I thought about Chuck's comment on 'pushing the button' and I made up folders with the Agent's names on the tab and added a folder for James Duffey.

Linda told me she takes her lunch break at noon every day. I was at her office at 11:30 a.m. and told her I just needed three personnel folders, just to verify information for WFO evaluations. I did not need to sign them out and I would be done before she leaves for lunch. She wrote down the three names on a pad and pointed to a desk where I could sit. When Linda gave me the folders, I shuffled the folders enough times in case anyone was closely watching. I spent my time on Duffy's folder writing down all his references on his background investigation and I checked for anything on the Jeep salvage investigation. There was nothing . I returned the files to Linda, thanked her and headed back to my office just before noon.

I spent a good part of the afternoon searching for the reference names in the FBI and Justice Department directories. I did it alphabetically and I wished I had started at the end of the alphabet. I think this may be the person we are looking for:

Associate Attorney General John G. Williams

Office Telephone 202-555-1835

I would like to make this the first topic for tomorrow's Zoom meeting."

Jim replied to George with a copy to all of us:
"You can count on it. It may be the only item on the agenda.

I am surprised you did not wait until 8:35 p.m. to send it.

Nice work!"

Enthusiasm surfaced again and the Zoom meeting started at 4:45 a.m.

Jim started the meeting again thanking George for 'pushing the button' and moving the case forward, and everyone applauded.

George immediately responded with, "I hope that wasn't premature. I am not 100 percent sure yet. His cell phone will tell us more than his office phone and we do not have his cell number yet.

Joe responded, "You give me his home address and two passes by his house, and I will have all his cell numbers. Do you have his address?

George replied, "He lived in Dumfries, Virginia fifteen years ago."

Jim interjected, "I can take care of all of this. WATCH24 has a contract with a company that will tell us all there is to know about him by the end of the day. I will call them when we finish the meeting.

Joe said, "I think the next obstacle will be getting his office and cell phone records. Jim can that company of yours tell us which vendor has the contract for DOJ office phones, cell phones and internet service.

Jim was quick to answer, "For what we pay them each month, they should be able to tell us the color of his underwear. I will get every bit of information they have."

"We are still lacking any evidence of a crime, so we have more work to do," Steve added. "I do not want to lower the standards and have a "fishing expedition" or we will be as corrupt as the FBI and the January 6th Commission."

I said, "We still need to locate the driver of the blue Jeep Cherokee and right now, we do not know if it is a man or a woman. To begin, this person is the key and wants to help us and see the shooter and others arrested. And that is why he/she is giving us clues. That person may have experience as a paid police informant, and now we know that person may have a slight limp. For me that says we may be looking for a former law enforcement officer who retired on a disability. We need to find an honest supervisor in the FBI Washington Field Office that can help us. "

"I am probably the best one to follow up on this." George offered. "Today I will pull personnel files for recent disability retirements. And Saturday, I will talk in confidence to Agent Lawton and Holland at the safe house and see if they can help us."

Tom also offered to call Agent Henry Parson from the Tulsa Office and see if he can help us.

"Given the history of the President and his son, I would not rule out that our players may somehow be tied to a foreign government," General Monroe stated. "Normally, we would have checked with the Office of the Director of National Intelligence and received an answer, but that is clearly out of the question. What a sad situation when you can no longer trust the federal government."

Jim, looking somber, said, 'I want all of us to be clear on this. I want everyone to text the group with every piece of information we find on this and everything we discussed today. If you have documents, scan them and send them to Steve and then seal your originals in evidence bags and hand deliver them to Steve.

Steve, when you feel we have enough to subpoena phone records or any other records, initiate a group conference call and we will figure out our next step. "

Judge Walters added, "There is one point I need to emphasize. We learned from the Sanchez case, and it shows in all the precautions we are taking. This time, I will not be signing any subpoenas, search warrants or arrest warrants. That is why I have recruited three honest and experienced judges. They have no knowledge of this groups' actions or anything about the case. They are aboard to supervise the grand jury or grand juries should there be a need, make decisions on subpoenas and warrants, and for pretrial arraignments. And if three are inadequate, I have three more ready to serve. This allows me to stay with the group and help the entire process run smoothly."

The meeting ended with Jim saying, "All our plates are full. Let's get to work."

After breakfast, I went to my study and reviewed my notes from the meeting. I was hoping that we could produce the driver quickly and that he or she really wanted to help us and wouldn't immediately "lawyer up." And then, I paused and thought, what dream world am I living in? I rapidly dismissed my negativity and thought, perhaps the Lord will give us another path.

I did not think it would take very long for Jim's company to find Attorney General Williams and I was right. At 2:15 p.m., Jim sent the following text message to the group:

"Assistant Attorney John Gerald Williams lives at 1702 Maple Avenue in Vienna, Virginia. I have a data sheet on him which will be on your laptop in about fifteen minutes. I saw nothing unusual."

A few minutes later, Joe sent the following text message:
"I will wait to about eleven this evening to drive past his home. That way I am quite sure all their cell phones will be there. I will send you the numbers and they will be on your phone awaiting when you crawl out of bed tomorrow morning."

I got up just before 6:00 a.m. and made a pot of coffee, just like I always do whether Kim is here or not. I poured myself a cup and grabbed my phone and went to my study.

At 1:25 in the early morning, Joe sent us the text message he promised:

"Good morning.

Nice two-story brick front house with a security system and a ring doorbell. I did not detect any other cameras. The home phone number is on the data sheet that Jim sent us earlier. John and his wife, Sara live in the home.

There were three cell phones in the home:

703-555-4218

703-555-4219

571-555-2241

I am going to assume that the top two phones are John's and Sara's although I do not know which one belongs to John. The third phone also has a Vienna area code that tells me it was purchased within the last thirty-two months when they added the additional area code. Given my expert CIA training, I think it is safe to say that the third number is the one that should capture our interest.

Enjoy your day."

That's typical Joe. He always gives it to you straight with just a touch of humor.

George's search for recent disability retirements in the Washington Field Office and the Tulsa Office on Friday did not give us any leads as to the identity of the driver. He told everyone that he would text us tomorrow after interviewing Agents Lawton and Holland.

Tom Wilson left a message on Agent Henry Parson's home

phone, but most likely would not get a response until tonight or tomorrow.

There wasn't much for me to do now on the case , so I decided to gas both our cars before the prices went any higher. On my second trip to the gas station with Kim's car, I stopped at the grocery store for the usual milk, bread, cereal and fruit. On the way home, I picked up a sub sandwich for dinner.

Inflation is hitting all of us. That morning outing cost me over $150—$110 dollars for filling two cars that each had more than a quarter of a tank of gas, $36 for one bag of groceries and over $8 dollars for a sub. I know that this is hitting the middle class the hardest. This President is destroying America, and no one will convince me that it is not intentional.

I briefly spoke to Jim in the late afternoon and neither one of us had much to add to the case. But we did have one accomplishment; all was not lost as we decided to meet at one of our favorite restaurants at 5:00 p.m. for an early dinner on Saturday. It was obvious that we both missed having our wives by our side.

I spent the evening catching up on the latest news by finally reading today's paper and watching the news on television. I watched 30 minutes of one of the "main street media" channels to see what they were lying about today. Then I switched to one of the cable channels in my quest for something closer to the truth. If the media was the fourth leg of our democracy, our three-legged stool was wobbling and about to tip over.

Friday night in America and I was under the covers by 10:00 p.m.

"Freedom is never more than one generation away from extinction. We didn't pass it to our children in the bloodstream. It must be fought for, protected, and handed on for them to do the same, or one day we will spend our sunset years telling our children and our children's children what it was once like in the United States where men were free."
—Ronald Reagan

CHAPTER 27

The buzzing and flashing of my cell phone took me out of a deep sleep. It was 2:25 a.m. and I saw it was an emergency conference call. As soon as everyone was connected General Monroe gave us the news:

"At exactly 2:00 a.m., New York City's electric grid was shut down by a cyberattack and most of the city and parts of the suburbs are without power. Both the Governor and the Mayor will be declaring a State of Emergency in the next ten minutes or so. The National Guard is being mobilized to assist the New York City Police and the State Police.

The timing tells us much. Seventy-five to eighty percent of

the people are still asleep now. I am not downplaying the severity of this; we will still have multiple deaths and it is an act of war. But whoever is responsible is assessing the will of our President, the readiness of our emergency services and our military and the strength of our resolve.

Sit tight and I will be texting updates throughout the morning."

I will tell you how I see this. The President has turned America into a ninety-pound weakling lying on the beach and the bully just kicked sand in our face.

After watching the weak and indecisive actions of our President and military brass during the Afghanistan withdrawal, which was the largest military screw-up in American history, I am surprised they waited this long to evaluate us.

Now we are witnessing both foreign and domestic attacks on America at the same time.

At 4:10 a.m., we received an update stating that there were reports of multiple deaths in NYC hospitals, nursing homes and a lesser number of deaths from traffic accidents. 911 emergency calls were increasing each hour. All first responders will be working twelve-hour days. All air traffic in and out of NYC has been terminated.

At 5:10 a.m. we received another conference call from General Monroe:

"Another 2:00 a.m. Pacific Daylight Time cyberattack on the power grid in Los Angeles. The entire city and a large part of Los Angeles County are without electricity. There is no difference between the two attacks. Deaths are already being reported in LA. Both the Mayor and the Governor will be declaring a State of Emergency. I have heard that the President is about to leave his beach home and return to the White House, but I have no confirmation on this. Updates to follow when necessary."

The only positive thought I now have is the fact that it will be daylight in New York very shortly.

At 7:00 a.m., Jim sent a text message that there would be an emergency Zoom meeting at 7:30 a.m.

I was already up and dressed and watching the news. The pundits hit the ground running with statements that would surely cause panic throughout the world:

"Is this the start of World War III?"

"Armageddon in America,"

"New York, then LA; Is Washington, DC next?"

"Experts estimate thousands of deaths."

"America is Under Attack."

"Europe is preparing for cyberattacks."

The White House released the following statement:

"Early this morning America experienced two cyberattacks on our power grids, one in New York City and one in Los Angeles. Both governors and both mayors have declared States of Emergency. I have spoken to both governors and offered federal resources as needed. The Federal Bureau has launched an investigation and is assisting law enforcement at both locations.

I ask that everyone remain calm and pray for our country. I assure you that those responsible for these attacks will not go unpunished."

The General opened the Zoom meeting with an update.

"Actually, the public is calmer than what you would believe from watching the news. There is nothing our group can do now except pray for America.

Pure and simple, a 2:00 a.m. cyberattack in New York City and another one at 2:00 a.m. in Los Angeles were intentionally "soft" for a reason. We can expect over a thousand deaths, but it could have easily been ten thousand if it occurred at 8:00 a.m. on a weekday morning. The initial press release from the White House was lame, and I urge you pay close attention to any statement from the White House, the President or the Pentagon. There is more to this than meets the eye. I will be updating you regularly."

Jim added, "The news coverage of this will be on every channel for most of the day. I have eight WATCH24 agents at Headquarters listening and recording all the news on the attacks. Today 'everyone and their brother' will be making comments. If you see or hear anything strange or unusual, note the channel and time so we can look at it later. Paul Harvey would always say, 'And that is the rest of the story.' That is our goal, uncover the rest of the story.

Joe and George do not change your plans to head on out to the safe house so you can assure everyone that they have nothing to be worried about.

Chuck, we are still having dinner tonight at 5:00 p.m. and if any of you want to join us, give me a call."

As the meeting ended, I thought how fortunate we were to have General Monroe in our group. He has extensive experience in national intelligence and still serves as a consultant to countries throughout the free world. And the fact that he believes this "does not pass the smell test," is all Jim needed to start capturing all the news coverage for dissection.

This is most definitely not a normal Saturday, but it was a quiet one. As I was watching the news, I listened to many, so-called "experts" on cyberterrorism, I had to make one observation. If there are all these experts throughout our government and private sector, why is it so easy to attack our electric grids?

At 11:30 a.m., there was a group message from Tom Wilson:

"I finally got a call from FBI Agent Henry Parsons this morning. After we discussed the cyberattacks for a few minutes, I described the person we are looking for." He paused and said, "'This is a long shot, but this may help.'"

He went on to explain that there was a CIA agent assigned to the Tulsa Joint Terrorism Task Force named David (Dave) Wilcox. Duffy and Wilcox were teamed up and they became good friends. One night after a long day at work, Wilcox was driving home when he was hit head-on by a drunk driver. No one thought he would live, but he did. His one leg was so crushed it had to be amputated. He had a long recovery ahead of him. When he was released from rehab, Duffy invited him to stay in his home since Wilcox was divorced and lived in a second-floor apartment. As a result, they became even better friends.

Wilcox had no choice but to take a full disability retirement from the federal government. That devastated him since the CIA was his whole life. He did not need the money due to a large settlement, but he missed the work. Duffy helped him find a few temporary positions as a paid drug undercover informant in local police departments. But after he testified several times in open court, no department would touch him.

I asked Henry if he knew where Wilcox was now. He told me that the last he knew, Wilcox and his physical therapist were living together. He did not know her name but told me he would do a check and get back to me early in the week. After hearing this, I think we found our guy.

I will update you as soon as Henry gets back to me."

After reading the message, I just sat in the den in silence and digested all I had just read. I first thanked the Lord. If this in not Divine Intervention, I don't know what is. And if Wilcox was sending us clues, I do believe that he will tell us everything. For at least the next five minutes, I never gave one thought to the cyberattacks.

I skipped lunch since Jim and I were dining out tonight and decided I needed a nap so I would be able to hold my head erect during dinner.

My phone woke me at 2:35 p.m. It was Jim.

"Chuck, I have Joe and George on the line also. Go ahead Joe."

Joe stated, "What a day. To begin, everyone here is fine and our talk lowered everyone's anxiety level.

Mark and Bill Holland pulled us aside and asked if they could ride back with us and help us with the investigation. Quite honestly, they both have 'cabin fever.' Mark's gunshot wound is healed to the point that no bandage is required. I spoke to Ann and asked if he could return to work. Her response was, 'That would be fine if you don't let him get shot again.'

I am sure we could use them. What do you think?"

Jim immediately responded, "Bring them back. We could use the help. Mark cannot go home, so Joe, can he stay with you?"

Joe replied, "Sure, I could use an assistant. I liked him from the first time I met him." And we all laughed.

George added, "That text message from Tom sounds promising. We will have a lot to discuss Monday morning. And Diane wanted to thank everyone for all the concern and keeping all the families safe."

Jim commented, "We are all one big family and are glad you and Diane are a part of it."

Tom is going to join Chuck and me for dinner tonight. Will you two be back in time to join us?"

"Not this time, Joe replied. "The ladies are going to have an early dinner for us before we head back."

"Enjoy your time with them and have a safe trip," Jim said as the call ended.

The restaurant was crowded and our table was in the center, so we did not discuss the case all evening. At 6:10 p.m., the three of us all reached for our phone at the same time. There was a text from General Monroe:

> *"Electric power has been restored to New York City. I expect Los Angeles will have power restored in three hours. Very Interesting."*

We all looked at each other and no one said a word.

We enjoyed a nice dinner and as we were walking to our cars, Jim said, "Let's all digest this and any further information we receive from General Monroe and we will talk tomorrow."

At 9:10 p.m., we received the anticipated text message from General Monroe telling us that electric power had been restored to Los Angeles. He also said that the President will be addressing the nation sometime Monday morning.

Sunday morning, I got up in time to go to early church. I had a desire and an obligation to thank and praise the Lord for the guidance He has given all of us.

Jim sent Tom and me a text message at 9:15 a.m.:

"Just to let you know, I decided to fly out to the compound and surprise Patricia with a picnic lunch before it gets crazy here. Call me if anything urgent surfaces. We can continue our case conversation tomorrow."

Jim is right. If Wilcox is our guy, it will be busy here and timing becomes important. And I do think Jim needs a break.

There is so much recent and varied information, I needed to spend most of the afternoon sorting through it and listing the questions that I need answered. The way I view it, especially after reading Jim's text message, is that when all hell breaks loose, any work I do now will make life easier later.

Late in the afternoon, I had an enjoyable conversation with Kim, Marie and Katherine who all were in high spirits. I also called Jason to check on him and suggested that next weekend we visit our family. That raised his spirits and gave him something to look forward to. And I also spoke to Tom and Sharon. They told me they worked all weekend and were glad to be home relaxing. The word "baby" was never spoken.

The Monday morning Zoom meeting started at 4:45 a.m. again. General Monroe opened with an update on the cyberattacks.

"There were 865 deaths in New York City and 683 deaths in Los Angeles reported as related to the sixteen-hour power outage. Those figures will change throughout the week as autopsies are completed and more people are reported as not responding to phone calls or missing.

These were well-planned cyberattacks and to control them with exact times tells me that someone in the United States was part of the operation. Jim and I spoke yesterday, and this morning's presidential address and all comments will be recorded and later analyzed. There is something amiss in all of this and I will not rest until we uncover it. Pay close attention to the address. I am predicting it will not be what we are expecting."

Jim told the group that Agent Mark Lawton has recovered from the gunshot wound and he and Agent Bill Holland will now be working with us on the investigation.

Tom referred to the text message he sent Saturday and commented that he believes that the case will depend on Dave Wilcox's cooperation and honesty. It could break the case wide open or set us back to ground zero.

He stated, "If he does cooperate, I am concerned for his life. If this case is anything close to what I am envisioning, we need to take every precaution possible. I would never send him to the compound, and to place him in jail as a material witness is a death sentence. What we need is a fortified safe place close to the grand jury."

Jim responded, "Consider it done."

As soon as I heard Jim's words, I knew two things. The safe house that Tom was requesting, already exists and there would no further discussion on it.

Steve spoke next and said, "For discussion and planning, let us assume that Wilcox is the witness we want him to be. Joe, can we get Assistant AG Williams' phone records without raising a red flag?"

"Yes, as long as we have the numbers and the service provider and I hand deliver the subpoena," Joe replied.

Jim assured him that he would have the information sometime this morning.

Steve continued, "Subpoena requests for bank records, correspondence, memos, emails, calendars and more could take months. Any request for these types of records will be managed by search warrants for offices and homes. We can then issue subpoenas for the records we do not have."

This issue raised some questions about logging and securing evidence. Jim offered to assign two WATCH24 agents full time to the evidence room. George stated he would provide copies of the FBI evidence procedures manual for guidance.

Steve ended with, "We still do not have a specific crime. Does anyone have an idea what that may be?"

General Monroe responded, "Give me several days. Does treason work?"

Steve replied, "That works perfectly for me General."

And the Monday morning Zoom meeting was ended.

It was noon before the President stepped up to the podium to address the nation. Standing behind him were the Vice President, the Attorney General, the Secretary of State, the Secretary of Defense, and the Secretary of Homeland Security. What I found strange was the Director of National Intelligence was missing.

In part, the President's address follows:

"My fellow Americans,
We have just experienced the worst cyberattack that America
has ever faced. My sympathy and condolences to the families
of the fifteen hundred families who lost loved ones during this

unprovoked attack. They will never be forgotten. The assistance we received from countries throughout the world was heartwarming. The Canadian government offered help for New York City and the Mexican government offered help for Los Angeles. But I would be remiss if I did not recognize the President of the People's Republic of China for all he has done for our country. There was a call yesterday from China to the Secretary of State stating they had irrefutable evidence that the government of Iran was responsible for the cyberattacks on New York City and Los Angeles. I called President Xi Jinping this morning and personally thanked him for all his help. To show how much he genuinely cared and wanted to protect his partnership with America, he told me that at noon Eastern Standard Time, China would launch a cyberattack on the Iranian power-grid in retaliation for what they did to America. Folks, you could not ask for a better friend than that."

I couldn't believe what I was hearing. I went to my study and picked up my phone to initiate a call and saw a group message from General Monroe:

"That was a better speech than you think. Sit tight and do not comment on the speech. I will get back to you in thirty minutes."

Now I am as confused as ever. I know and trust General Monroe well enough to do exactly what he told me to do, sit tight. That task is much more difficult to follow than I thought. I went back into the den and watched the commentators praising the President for his leadership and strength during the crisis. It was so sickening that I turned off the television and sat there in total shock.

My phone rang twenty minutes later and I was relieved that it was a conference call from General Monroe.

"Let me start by telling you this is top-secret information that can never be repeated, but you have the need to know. As soon as I heard the first few minutes of the President's address, I knew it was a 'dog and pony' show. I am listening in one ear and calling my contact in Israel in the other. As soon as we both heard the President finish praising China, I asked him to pay close attention. I said we both know that China is not going to launch a cyberattack of any significance on Iran. So, if Israel were to initiate a devastating cyberattack on the power grid that supports their nuclear facility, how could Iran blame any other country but China. If China states that wasn't us, it was Israel, they would lose their credibility and any good will they hoped to gain from this scam. China would have to force Iran to remain silent since China just promised the world, they were going to cyberattack Iran in retaliation for the attack on America. Even in his declining cognitive state, our President knows if this gets out, he will be gone within a month. What he does not know is that his days are numbered no matter what happens. It is a win-win situation for us and it will be years before Israel will have to be concerned about Iran having nuclear capabilities. They certainly made a huge mistake here that left an opportunity that we will never see again.

He told me he would get back to me in fifteen to twenty minutes. That is when I texted the group message to all of you.

He did get back to me and said he had approval for the cyberattack on the electric grid that supports Iran's nuclear facility. If it hasn't been completed by now, it won't be very much longer. My guess is that you will never hear a word about it. Now you know why I called and did not send a text message.

And thank you again, Mister President."

I only have one thing to say. Brilliance always trumps stupidity.

"I have cherished the ideal of a democratic and free society in which all persons will live together in harmony and with equal opportunities. It is an ideal which I hope to live for and to see realized. But, my lord, if needs be, it is an ideal for which I am prepared to die."
—Nelson Mandela

CHAPTER 28

We won an important battle yesterday, thanks to General Monroe. But we still have work to do before we can declare a victory.

I would like to believe that Dave Wilcox cares about America, but I am having a tough time reconciling this with his participation in a felony assault on an FBI Agent. I cannot think of any possible scenario that is plausible and would justify his criminal behavior. Yet, it appears that he was sending clues to us that would lead to an arrest. In any case, I hope Tom hears from Henry today or tomorrow, because currently, everything is at a standstill.

After breakfast, I watched the news. The praise of the President continued, but because I knew the truth, I did not find it sickening; I found it humorous. However, after ten minutes, it was sickening again and I turned it off and went to my study.

I spent time reviewing all my notes checking to assure we had all we needed to move forward. Jim sent a text message yesterday to the group with all the information for phone record subpoenas and included the name and phone number for the head of security, who is retired from the FBI and had worked with Jim in the past.

After the President's address yesterday, I would hope Steve has the crime he needs and I hope it is treason.

After completing the full review, I was right back where I started. We need to talk to Dave Wilcox.

After another hour at my desk, I became a bit impatient and called Tom to see if he had heard from Henry.

Tom picked his phone up on the first ring and said, "Chuck, I am one step ahead of you. I already called Henry." And we both laughed.

"Sorry," I said. "I couldn't help myself."

Tom replied,"I understand. After yesterday, I just want this case to get moving. Henry told me he would try to track down Wilcox today and call me late this afternoon no matter what the outcome."

"You can't ask for more than that," I added and then I followed up with a question.

"Can you think of any scenario where a retired CIA officer would be driving a vehicle during a felony assault on an FBI agent?"

Tom answered, "No. I have had the same thought. I am not sure how Wilcox will explain this one. But we need for him to be honest with us or we are back to ground zero. "

I closed the call by saying, "Exactly, my point. Please let me know when you hear from Henry."

I felt better knowing Henry was trying to locate Wilcox. I realize every step takes time and I decided to find something else to do to occupy mine.

Kim wanted another shelf in the pantry. So, I took some measurements, went to Lowe's and by 4:00 p.m., there was a new empty white shelf in the pantry awaiting groceries.

Tom called at 4:45 p.m. "We are making progress. Henry told me he could not locate Wilcox, but he was able to talk to Janice Kilmer, his therapist live-in girlfriend. He told her he had good news for Dave on a job and needs to contact him ASAP. She told Henry he is away working out of town for a month or so, but he is always available for a call after ten in the evening and she gave Henry his number, which is 539-555-2726."

I replied, "Tom that's great news. I need to talk to Jim and Joe. Can you be at my house at 9:00 p.m. this evening?"

Tom answered, "Sure, see you then."

I made a conference call to Jim and Joe and brought them up to date and then said, "Our safety and Wilcox's safety is my primary concern. My plan right now is to have Joe, Tom and Steve at my home and make the call to Wilcox on an untraceable phone and see what he offers. However, if he agrees, we would rather have a face-to-face with him, if possible, before we go any further.

Joe, I am going to need the phone and the recording device from you and I will text you Wilcox's cell phone number.

Currently, we have too many unanswered questions. Is he staying alone? Is he staying with Duffy? Does he have a tracker on his car? Is this a set up?"

Joe suggested, "Since you are not calling him until 10:00 p.m.

and we have Duffy's address, on my way to your home, I will do a pass by and get plate numbers and all the cell phone numbers in the house. If I see the opportunity, I will also check the cars for tracking devices."

Jim added, "Remember we do have a safe house in the area if you need it. As soon as we hang up, I will have my contractor do a file dump on Wilcox and see what they can find. Let's do a full conference call at 9:00 p.m. and discuss strategies. I will put a notice out."

This is exactly what I was concerned about. An hour ago, I was idle with nothing to do. Now my plate is overloaded and only have an abbreviated time to do my homework.

Jim called me back in less than five minutes. I answered the phone immediately, "Chuck, after thinking on this, I would feel better if your son, Tom and Agent Bill Holland were covertly in the house, probably upstairs someplace, just in case you need any help. Tom told me he could put his car in a driveway down the street. Talk to you at nine."

Jim is thorough and cautious and I would feel better also.

Tom Wilson was at my door at 8:10 p.m. My son Tom and Bill were here at 8:20 with a dozen donuts in case it was a long meeting. Joe was here by 8:50 with the phone and recorder.

Joe opened with, "This is going to be a little more difficult than we had hoped. Wilcox is at Duffy's house. Let me get this recorder set up and I will fill everyone in during the conference call.

The conference call began on time. Jim started with, "From everything I read in the report I received, David Michael Wilcox appears to be a law-abiding, altruistic, decent human being. He did receive a huge settlement from the accident and does not need to work. It looks like he spends most of his time volunteering with his church and community. He is on the Board of Directors for the local Boys and Girls Club and he has been recognized by the community with numerous awards and commendations. He has lived in the same small house for years. The only thing I saw that was odd is that he owns a 2013 Honda SUV, which has plates that expired two months ago."

Joe said, "I can probable explain that. Most likely Dave has been here working with Duffy for the last two months and was letting his registration expire until he returned home.

On my pass by I detected four cell phones at Duffy's residence. One is Wilcox's, I assume the second phone is Duffy's FBI phone based on the number, the third is likely Duffy's wife phone. The fourth you will find most interesting, 571-555-2242, the twin of Department of Justice Attorney John G. Williams' cell phone. Good news for us, dumb move by them.

The rental car in the driveway, closest to the road is a dark gray Hyundai SUV which has a tracking device and I believe is the vehicle that Wilcox drives. I am now 'waving the caution flag.' Tom Wilson did not hesitate to state, "After hearing all this, my suggestion is that we go ahead with the 10:00 p.m. call to Wilcox and when completed, have another conference call to discuss our next move."

Everyone agreed. It looks to me like it is going to be a long night.

We spent the next half-hour composing the script for the phone call to Wilcox, knowing that what we say in those few minutes, will either make our case, or God forbid, destroy everything we have accomplished in the last twenty-four hours.

The call was made at 10:10 p.m.

The phone rang three times before Wilcox answered and said, "Hello."

I started by reading from the script, "Dave, this is Chuck Burke, and we know you are an honest law-abiding man who could use our help."

Wilcox responded, "Thank you for returning my call, Doctor Farrell. I have been having so much severe pain in my hip that I thought I would die. Can I come to your office tomorrow morning to see you?"

There was a short pause and before I could go back to my script, I heard him say, "Thank you, "8:00 o'clock works for me and I will bring my medical records. You are in suite 204 in the medical building next to the hospital, correct?" And there was another short pause. "Thank you again, and I will see you at eight in the morning." And with that, he ended the call.

Joe commented, "His script was a hell of a lot better than ours." You can tell he was a CIA agent. He told us everything we need to know in a fake thirty-second call from his doctor."

Agent Bill Holland stated, "I can't wait to see his so-called medical records."

Chuck's son Tom added, "I already googled the doctor; her name is Janice Farrell and she does specialize in pain management. Wilcox had the correct address for her office."

Tom Wilson said, "And Wilcox thinks his life is in jeopardy."

Before we initiated the group conference call, I asked one question, "Is there anyone in this room who thinks we should not be at Doctor Farrell's office tomorrow morning at 7:45 a.m.?" No one said a word.

We started the conference call by playing the recording of the call to Dave Wilcox.

Jim was first to respond, "Wow, this guy is good. We could not have asked for anything more."

There was a lengthy discussion on the strategy for tomorrow's meeting with everyone's safety being the main concern. We finally decided to have Tom and Bill in the parking lot watching Dave's car and looking for any other questionable activity. Tom Wilson and Sharon will be sitting in the lobby watching the main door. Chuck and Joe will be outside Suite 204 waiting for Dave. Once Dave appears, Joe will hand him a note that says, "DO NOT TALK. IF YOU HAVE YOUR CELL PHONE, TURN IT OFF AND HAND IT TO ME." If he hands the phone to Joe, it will be placed in a lead-lined bag and everyone will be able to speak openly.

On the east end of the building on the first floor, there is a small lounge where hopefully they can have a private discussion. Steve will be there waiting for them.

Jim concluded with, "The safe house is stocked and ready. If you need it. Tom and Bill will take Dave there, but if we can delay it just one more day, it will make a dramatic difference in our case. Looks like we have a plan, so get some sleep and stay safe tomorrow."

It was close to midnight by now and I told everyone they could crash here if they did not want to drive home. Tom elected to go home since he lived only ten minutes from me. Bill went home since had been away from his family for so long when he was at the safe house with Mark. The remainder found a spot to get comfortable and no one complained.

"For you have been called to live in freedom, my brothers and sisters. But don't use your freedom to satisfy your sinful nature. Instead, use your freedom to serve one another in love."
—Galatians 5:13

CHAPTER 29

Breakfast consisted of coffee, orange juice and the donuts Tom brought last evening.

Everyone was at their designated stations by 7:50 a.m. We were ready and a bit anxious. As Dave Wilcox approached us, we noted that he was carrying a file folder in his left hand. Joe immediately put his finger to his lips. As Dave offered a handshake, Joe put the note in his hands. Dave smiled and said, "You guys are good, and my phone is locked in the glovebox of my rental car."

We all shook hands and Joe said, "You did an excellent job on that phone call last night. You told us everything we needed to know. I assume the pain is much better this morning."

With a smile, Dave said, "The pain is gone now that we are talking. I can't tell you how long I have been waiting for this meeting. Is there someplace we can talk in private?"

"We have it all set up and I see you brought your medical file," I said.

"Yes, I did," Dave replied. "And I can't wait to show it to you."

We moved down to the first floor lounge where Steve introduced himself.

Steve opened by saying, "Before we get down to business, there is one barrier we must remove. Tell us about the two shootings."

Dave, appearing to be genuinely concerned, started by saying, "First can I ask you how Agent Mark Lawton is doing?" Chuck told him that Mark has fully recovered and is back to work.

Dave responded, "Thank the Lord, that was not intentional.

Let me start from the beginning. Jim Duffy, who has been a longtime friend since we both served on the Joint Terrorism Task Force in Tulsa, offered me a contract position to help him with a special investigation on corruption in the FBI and other federal agencies. I missed working for the CIA so I took the position even though I had to work in the Washington DC area. I really did not need the income, but he paid me $7,500 and provided a vehicle, which is a whole other story. On my first day in Washington, Jim introduced me to Assistant Attorney General John Williams, who oversaw the investigation and the Director of the FBI. Jim has always exaggerated his importance, but after the introductions to such high-level bosses, I thought this was all true. In fact, on the way out the door of Williams' office, I grabbed his card and that is why everything was happening at 8:35 p.m."

Joe added, "And thank you, that is exactly what led us to you."

Dave continued, "Good to know as that was my intent."

As time passed, and the more that we got into this case, the more I thought there was another agenda here that I knew nothing about. I started to ask questions and Duffy's answers were so evasive and self-serving, that I changed from supporting this alleged investigation to investigating the entire charade and the evidence of my findings are in this folder." And Dave held up the folder.

Dave continued, "I assume that Duffy realized he was losing his credibility with his peers, so he came up with the plan to scare those corrupt agents who were interfering with our investigation. When he told me his plan to shoot into agent's homes, I told him that I wanted nothing to do with it. He told me that if I refused his order, he would fire me. Now I had a dilemma. I did not have enough evidence to stop this treasonous charade, but if I reverted to my CIA tactics, I might be able to make this work. I went to Jim and told him we have been friends too long and he was there for me when I needed him and so I wanted to be there for him when he needs me. I told him if you let me handle this operation, I will take care of it and no one will get hurt. He agreed. The shooter in the Jeep was Skip Stone, who was a local police officer or deputy sheriff in southern Maryland and was fired for assaulting a prisoner. I am not sure how Jim knows him, but as far as I know, this is the only time he used him.

Duffy provided the 9MM for the shooting. Once I knew that, I provided the ammunition for the weapon. For the shootings, I loaded the magazine with an unjacketed round with reduced powder and a frangible bullet for the second round. I wanted to make sure the first round broke at least a two-pane window. Both times the weapon only had two rounds loaded. Since both homes are slightly elevated from the road, I told Skip to aim at the top of the window so the round would end up in the ceiling. The forensic unit should have only located one slug in each home.

I feel horrible about Agent Lawton getting injured. I can only assume that the reduced powder let the slug fall after it broke the window. I going to ask for two things. First, I want to apologize to the Lawton family and somehow make it better knowing I can never make it right. And secondly, I want to be the person who puts the handcuffs on Duffy. He certainly was not the friend to me that I was to him, and I want him to know that he is nothing more than a rotten treasonous bastard who needs to spend his remaining years in prison. And I will be happy that I helped put him away, and if necessary, I will die trying, because, unlike him, I remain loyal to my country and my oath."

Dave asked, "What other questions do you have for me?"

We asked him about the dark blue Jeep Cherokee. Dave stated, "That was a shock to me. I asked Jim if this was the same Jeep that he drove when he was assigned to the Joint Terrorism Task Force. He smiled and said it sure is and I got it for one thousand dollars. This was my first indication that Jim is not the person I thought he was."

In closing, I said, "First, I want to assure you that we will do everything we can to fulfill your two requests. But now let's talk about the next several days. You realize that if they knew you were talking to us, they would do everything within their power to kill you."

Dave replied, "I have known that for several weeks now."

Chuck continued, "What if Doctor Farrell told you that she is putting you in ICU for tonight and tomorrow you are being scheduled for several medical tests to include a full body scan and an MRI. And if all the tests are okay, you can tell Duffy that you will be back to work on Friday morning. However, you will actually be in a safe house with guards and as a bonus, you will receive a free sightseeing tour to a secret grand jury."

Dave had a quizzical look on his face and asked, "Can you possibly make that happen?"

Joe responded, "We already did. All you have to say is 'let's go.'"

"Let's go," Dave said, "What else do I need to do?"

Joe reached into his pocket and took out a phone and handed it to Dave. "This is your new phone; it is exactly like the one you left in the glove box except we can remotely control all incoming calls. If Jim calls you, the phone will ring in the ICU nurses' station and he will be told that no cell phones are allowed in ICU rooms. Simple rule—only approved calls will be sent to this phone. If this phone rings, answer it no matter what time day or night. One more thing, do not worry if Janice does not call you at 10:00 p.m. We will be dropping her off at the safe house to be with you by midnight."

Dave was shocked, "Now you're playing with me."

Joe responded, "We do not know you well enough to play with your mind yet. But don't worry, that day will come. And know that we always take life and death situations to heart and move them to the top of our 'to do' list. And that is what we did today."

I handed Dave a scripted message for the phone call to Duffy. We got another break. The phone went to Duffy's voice mail and Dave left the message. If he calls back, the call will go to the ICU nurses' station and will be answered by Tom's wife, Sharon, who is now an ICU nurse. Most times, good planning leads to success.

Dave thanked us profusely for our help saying we saved his life.

Who knows, perhaps we did.

I initiated a conference call as soon as Dave was on his way to the safe house. Joe and Chuck brought everyone up to date and you could almost hear the sigh of relief.

Steve followed by saying, "I have spent hours looking at the evidence folder that Dave provided. It is excellent and includes more high-ranking officials than I would have ever imagined. I asked the Judge to convene the grand jury as soon as possible. It is my understanding, and Judge correct me if I am wrong, with the help from Tony there are enough jurors from the panel to convene a grand jury at 1:00 tomorrow afternoon."

The Judge added, "More than enough. And we can continue it to Saturday if necessary."

Steve continued, "My goal is to get the main players locked up and off the street and once this is made public, we will have so many people wanting to testify, that we will have to give out numbers like they do at the deli counter. People are fed up with our federal government and once they feel it is safe to tell the truth once again, I believe this will be the largest corruption case in America's history. We will talk more on this at tomorrow mornings Zoom meeting."

Tom Wilson told everyone that he would call George this evening and tell him the good news.

I added, "I believe that George's days in FBI Headquarters are numbered."

Jim commented, "Two more at the most! I want to say how proud I am of each one of you. The toughest days are still ahead, so be sure to get a lot of rest tonight. Sleep may be fleeting for the next few days."

Jim opened the Thursday morning Zoom meeting with,

"This has been a hell of a week and it's not over yet. This morning we need to concentrate on our assignments and make sure we have all our bases covered. Where we find voids, we can fill them with WATCH24 personnel to free up sworn agents to make arrests."

George spoke up immediately, "I am sorry I missed yesterday. You can bet your bottom dollar I will be available when this case breaks. Before I left work last evening, I removed the few personal items I had in my office and brought them home. When you are ready to start making arrests, please call me immediately on my FBI cell phone and I will leave for an early lunch and never return to Headquarters."

Jim responded, "George, I have a better plan. Based on the evidence Steve now has in his possession, one of the initial warrants will be for the Director. Tom Wilson will come to your office and the two of you will go to the Director's office and you will make the arrest, so make sure your handcuffs are close by."

George said, "Thanks Jim. This will be the greatest day in my long FBI career."

Steve stated, "The evidence that Dave Wilcox provided us is going to shock America. We have an email with attachments and the distribution list that shows the total reorganization of the proposed federal 'social government' with charts and the names of those filling the new positions. They attempted to do this through personal email and computers, but it was sent to John Williams at DOJ who forwarded it to the White House.

"The four people we need to arrest at the same time are the FBI Director, the Attorney General, Assistant Attorney General

Williams and Agent Jim Duffy. The news will spread like a wildfire and create a panic throughout the federal government and the White House.

Agent Bill Holland and Tom Burke will make the arrests at the Department of Justice. And Jim Duffy is in for a surprise when he responds to the Mayflower Hotel to investigate another meeting of the 'Merry Gee's.

Starting next Monday, we will have two sitting grand juries to hear evidence on all those who are involved and indict all those that have committed a felony crime. And finally, there will be some high- level people who will be charged with treason."

Judge Walters spoke next. "We need to keep our federal government functioning without corruption, and I am counting on your help. Once the news breaks, I will be working with the congressional leadership to temporarily fill the agency heads that will soon be vacant. I have already spoken to Tom Wilson and he has agreed to serve as the Acting Attorney General. George, I am drafting you to be the acting FBI Director. And as vacancies occur, I will be asking all of you for recommendations."

Jim ended the meeting saying, "We all have much to do today, so does anyone have anything before we get back to work?"

"Yes," Joe quipped, "I have one comment. George do not expect a going away party when you leave. However, do not worry, I am certain they will throw you a party when you re-appear."

Joe's grin was infectious. All of us would have been disappointed if we did not hear a bit of humor from Joe. He always leaves a smile on our faces.

"Toil and Blood and Treasure, that it will cost Us to maintain this Declaration, and support and defend these States."
—John Adams, July 3, 1776

CHAPTER 30

With the additional help, the classification and logging evidence is now running smoothly. And both Steve and Tony are preparing the presentation and exhibits for this afternoon's grand jury meeting. I believe the criminal charges will keep flowing with the number of people who want to report what they know and others who will want to save their rear ends and are seeking a plea agreement.

So, I decided to spend my time today on the "administrative state" or better known the "deep state." An exceedingly difficult part of this investigation will be determining who in the deep state committed crimes and exactly what crimes they committed.

Robert W. Malone, MD, MS has written the best definition I have found:

> *"The "administrative state" is a general term used to describe the entrenched form of government that currently controls*

almost all levers of federal power in the United States, except for the Supreme Court of the United States (SCOTUS). The premature leaking of the SCOTUS majority decision concerning Roe v Wade to corporate press allies was essentially a preemptive strike by the administrative state in response to an action which threatened its power. The threat being mitigated was the constitutionalist logic upon which the legal argument was based, that being that authority to define rights not specifically defined in the US Constitution as being federally granted vests with individual states. Played out under the political cover of one of the most contentious political topics in modern US history, this was merely another skirmish demonstrating that the entrenched bureaucracy and its allies in the corporate media will continue to resist any constitutional or statutory restrictions on its power and privilege. Resistance to any form of control or oversight has been a consistent bureaucratic behavior throughout the history of the United States government, and this trend has accelerated since the end of the Second World War. More recently, this somewhat existential constitutionalist threat to the Administrative State was validated in the case of West Virginia vs. The Environmental Protection Agency, in which the court determined that when federal agencies issue regulations with sweeping economic and political consequences the regulations are presumptively invalid unless Congress has specifically authorized the action. With this decision, for the first time in modern history, boundaries have started to be imposed on the expansion of the power of unelected senior administrators within the Federal bureaucracy."

There will be search warrants issued for office and home computers, email records., office, home and cell phone records and all written correspondence for every person arrested. All this information will end up in a searchable data base which will automatically produce a list the names and numbers with the highest number (frequency). From that list, investigative leads will be assigned to agents which will result in additional arrests. Many deep state corrupt employees think they are invisible to law enforcement, but they are about to find out that is not true. It may take time, but they will be arrested. Their best chance to stay out of prison is come forward with information that will help the investigation and ask for a plea deal. The longer they wait, the higher the probability that they will go to prison and never see one dollar from their pension. The paranoia and constant fear that someone will ring their doorbell will take its toll, and they will learn that any benefits that they gained from their corrupt acts will be meaningless.

At 2:35 p.m., I received a phone call from Tom Wilson. I picked up my cell and said, "Congratulations, Tom. Are you ready for your new job?"

"Yes, and it's time to clean house." Tom said. "I am calling you because this morning when I decided to see what I could find on our shooter, Skip Stone, I googled him online and in the area newspapers. Spencer "Skip" Stone was found dead of an apparent suicide, in a field in Rockville, Maryland. I called Rockville Police Department and spoke to the case detective, Tim Preston. He told me he just received the gun shot residue test results from the lab and it came back negative. I told him that I had a deal for him. If he does not change the status to homicide for forty-eight hours, I will call him back and give him the name of the suspect before the time expires. He agreed since he is off the next two days, and gave me his cell phone number."

"That certainly gives us the advantage when we get to interrogate Duffy," I said.

Tom replied, "It sure does. I will call Steve and let him know."

My first thought was to thank God that we were able to move Dave and Janice to the safe house. My second thought was that Duffy must have seen Skip as a weak link and decided he could not take any chances.

It is Steve's decision as to when he will tell Dave. If it were me, I would tell him before he testifies, and my best guess is that Steve will do the same.

Back to my pile in the freezer for my dinner. I am down to my last few, but there is enough other food to keep me from starving to death. But that requires cooking, and I am not sure I am up to that challenge right now. I am going to make a major decision here. Tomorrow evening, I am going to order a pizza.

It was 9:00 p.m. by the time we received the conference call from Steve and Tony. Steve said, "We just finished our first grand jury session and it went very well. The jurors are all safely home, Dave is back at the safe house and we have four indictments.

I did tell Dave about Skip's death before he gave his testimony. He is one of the best witnesses I have seen in a long time. His ability to tell a story and his diligence made it easy for me. I only had one follow-up question. But more importantly, the jurors are very much like everyone else in America, and they want their country back and I think that sentiment will be the same during the criminal trials. And if the defense attorneys ask for a change in venue, it will not make any difference. For the first time in my career, I expect fewer trials and more pleas.

We have felony indictments for the Attorney General, the Director of the FBI, Assistant Attorney General John Williams and Agent James Duffy. And we have search warrants for all offices and homes of those arrested.

We have one more felony indictment for Agent Richard Barber for falsifying records. Steve is going to be with the group at the Mayflower Hotel tomorrow morning. We want Barber to see Duffy being arrested and handcuffed. Steve will take him to another room and show him the warrant. What he does and says after that will determine if he gets arrested or not."

"You both did an outstanding job," Jim told Steve and Tony. "Now let's fine tune our plan for tomorrow, so we make no mistakes, and no one gets hurt."

All arrests will take place at 9:00 a.m. Handcuff and search for weapons and empty all pockets. Place the prisoner in a chair away from his desk. If he tells you he wants an attorney do not say another word to him and at 9:15 a.m. let him make his call.

George will arrest the Director with Tom Wilson present.

Agent Bill Holland will arrest the Attorney General and the Assistant Attorney General (who will receive a call at 8:50 a.m. to report to the AG's office) with Tom Burke present.

Agent Mark Lawton will arrest Duffy with Steve, Joe and Chuck present

And Judge Waters has Judge Sullivan available for the initial arraignments and they will be committed without bail.

We have arranged for the United States Marshall Service to execute all the search warrants and work with our evidence team.

Bill Rounds and Janice Buckley will draft a press release and send it me for approval. It will not be released until after the arraignments. They will give us a synopsis of the weekend coverage at the Monday morning Zoom meeting.

Until we see how this plays out, there will be additional WATCH24 agents protecting you and your families. My advice is to stay home this weekend."

Good luck and stay safe. We will have a 2:00 p.m. Zoom meeting for any after-action comments and updates."

It is impossible to make three arrests in an office building without someone getting wind of it. So, as expected, someone informed the press that there were arrests being made in the Department of Justice and the quest for an exclusive story by the media began.

No one was surprised to see the Washington, DC media trucks parked on the streets surrounding the Justice Building, but by 11:00 a.m. it officially became a circus. There were at least thirty news vehicles and it was growing by the minute.

Without any real news, the rumors, and "unconfirmed source" stories were everywhere.

At 11:45 a.m., Jim initiated a text message to me, Steve, and our two media consultants, Bill Rounds and Janice Buckley:

> Jim stated the call by saying, "I am sure you are aware that every news agency is asking for a comment on the arrests made earlier today. The problem is the White House, the Department of Justice and the FBI are claiming they know nothing. The media cannot tie it to any federal law enforcement agency, so my suggestion is either do nothing or issue an inconsequential press release. Either option will

not stop the press from releasing their own 'exclusive story.' Review my draft let me know your thoughts by 5:00 p.m.

Draft Release (If needed):

Recently appointed Special Prosecutor Steven Mason, the former United States Attorney General, has announced the arrest of four unnamed officials from the Justice Department for felonies uncovered in an investigation of corruption in the federal government. The sensitivity of the ongoing investigation prohibits the release of names.

There will be a press conference on Monday afternoon which will provide the public with additional information.

Location and time of the press conference will be available at 10:00 a.m.

Jim opened the meeting exactly at 2:00 p.m. By stating, "I am anxious to hear how the arrests went, so George gsve us a summary of the FBI Director's arrest."

"It went better than I expected," George said. "Tom and I opened the door and walked right into the Director's office. He looked up and said, 'Excuse me, I am busy.'

I simply replied, 'Mr. Director, you are under arrest.'

He stated, 'You can't arrest me!'

Tom held out the warrant in front of his face and said, "Stand up and put your hands in the air." I handcuffed him, frisked him for weapons, emptied his pockets and sat him in a chair away from his desk, as planned.

Now he is yelling, 'I want to call my lawyer." Tom told him to give us a few minutes and we will let him make his call.

The Director's Secretary opened the door, stuck her head in and said, 'Oh my. Assistant Attorney General Williams is on the phone for the Director, but I will just tell him he is tied up,' and smiled at both of us and she closed the door.

I told the Director that both Williams and the Attorney General have also been arrested. He put his head down and kept saying 'No.'

The two Marshals entered the room and told the Director that they had search warrants for his office, his vehicles, and his home. He just kept shaking his head.

We left to take the Director to his arraignment, and the secretary pulled Tom aside and said, 'We have been waiting for this day; all of us knew he was destroying the FBI. I have been keeping documents that should help you,' and she held up a thick folder. Tom asked her to give it to the Marshals."

George commented, "And the award for the line of the day goes to the Director's secretary. And if that file is as damming as I think it is, I will make sure she is commended."

Jim stated, "That went well and is going to be a hard story to beat. Chuck, is your son, Tom with you?"

"I am here," Tom Burke said. "And ready to go."

"Agent Bill Holland and I just opened the door and walked into the Attorney General's Office. Assistant Attorney General Williams was sitting in a chair in front of the AG's desk.

Who in the hell are you and what do you want?' the Attorney General demanded.

Bill responded, 'I am FBI Agent Bill Holland and this is Tom Burke, and we have warrants for your arrests.' Williams bolted for the door, and I grabbed him just as the door opened. There stood a United States Marshall who said, 'Where do you think you are going?'

Bill told the Attorney General to stand up, raise his arms. And step away from his desk. Bill handcuffed him, frisked for weapons and emptied his pockets. I did the same with Assistant Attorney General Williams except I removed a Glock nine-millimeter semiautomatic from his waistband, rendered it safe and handed it to the US Marshall.

The Attorney General made his call to the Oval Office but was unable to get through. As you know Williams tried to call the FBI Director, but the Director was busy at that time. Bill told them that the FBI Director was also arrested.

The United States Marshall handed out copies of the search warrants for their offices, vehicles and homes. And we took them to their arraignments without any incident."

"Now we only have the Mayflower Hotel operation remaining. Joe, you're up," Jim said.

Joe began, "Our take down was a bit more complicated than the others. For those of you that had another assignment this morning, I want you to know that your digital twin filled in for you and did an excellent job.

We all arrived at the Mayflower Hotel at 8:15 a.m. At exactly 8:35 a.m., everyone please note the time, the check-in clerk in the lobby called Agent Duffy's cell phone, which is the same number on the card that Duffy gave the clerk on their first encounter. The clerk followed the script exactly as written: 'Agent Duffy, this is the clerk from the Mayflower Hotel. I thought you would like to know, that group you were interested in, the Merry Gee's, is having a meeting at 9:00 a.m. this morning in Room 205, the same room they used for earlier meetings. In fact, over half the people are here already. ' Duffy must have said, 'Thank you' because the Clerk ended the conversation with 'You are welcome.'

At 9:10 a.m., the WATCH24 agent in the lobby notified me that Agents Duffy and Barber arrived at the hotel. The WATCH24 agent followed them to the second floor and to room 205, just to make sure they did not draw their weapons before entering the room. They opened the door and walked in. Agent Duffy appeared shocked and started turning pale. I am not sure why but he did see FBI Agent Mark Lawton waiting for him. Mark stated, 'James Duffy, I have a warrant for your arrest. Raise your arms above your head and turn and face the wall.' Agent Lawton handcuffed him and the WATCH24 agent removed his service weapon, rendered it safe and Duffy was further searched for any additional weapons and everything was removed from his pockets.

FBI Agent Barber just stood still and watched. Chuck and Steve each grabbed one of his arms and moved him back to the hallway, where his service weapon was removed, he was handcuffed, searched and then placed in another vacant meeting room.

Duffy was put in a chair and Mark and I sat down next to him. He looked at both of us and said, "I need to make a phone call."

I said, 'Okay, who would you like to call'

"Assistant Attorney General John Williams," Duffy told me.

''You can't call him," I said. "He has been arrested along with the Attorney General and the FBI Director."

"Who can I call?" Duffy asked.

That was an interesting response; evidently Duffy's entire world was collapsing.

I said, "Jim, I really do not know who you should call. Think for a minute."

After a short pause, he said, "I want to call my friend, Dave Wilcox."

Mark and I looked at each other and I nodded my head. Both of us knew Duffy was at his breaking point and it was now or never.

I replied, "I am sorry, but you can't talk to Dave. He is busy right now."

Duffy was starting to panic and yelled, "Is he under arrest too?"

I said, "No, Dave is getting ready for his second appearance before a grand jury to testify against you."

Mark and I were surprised. We both though that would have broken him. But he gave us a second chance.

Duffy said, "I want to call my wife."

I replied, "We will have to check and see if she is free. Two United States Marshals are at your home now executing a search warrant."

He broke and put his head in his hands started crying. That is when I asked my last question.

"Jim, do you want to call Skip Stone?" Duffy raised his head with his eyes wide open and I added, "but you can't because you shot him."

"I didn't want to kill him, but Jack told me we had no other choice," Duffy blurted.

And that spontaneous utterance by Duffy was recorded on my body cam. Based on the expert police training I received from the CIA, I would say 'Jack' is Assistant Attorney General John G. Williams.

Let me end on this one thought. Throughout my career, I have learned that dirty cops break a lot easier than the usual everyday street felons. And I think the reason is that inside their corrupt, greedy minds, one moral speck has remained and surfaces when there is nothing left. I believe that Agent Duffy will tell us everything we need to know."

"Now we will hear the second part of the Mayflower Hotel operation from Steve," Jim said.

Steve started by commending the entire team saying he never expected the outcome from the initial arrests to generate this much information. "And the information keeps coming," Steve said. "And remember, it will be late in the evening before we start seeing the evidence collected by the United States Marshall's Service, and it will take us weeks to go through it.

Joe saved us a great deal of time and legal procedures by his initial interview with Agent Duffy. As soon as Chuck and I sat down with him, he apologized for his conduct and said he will tell us everything and testify in court if requested. His only request is that his family be protected and not suffer for his illegal actions.

Chuck and I brought Agent Richard Barber into an adjoining meeting room and showed him the warrant for falsifying records. Barber told us that he remembered that case because Jim Duffy and he had a disagreement on both the dates and times. It was a simple case for violation of federal probation due to possession of a firearm.

Barber said, "I knew I was right, and I did not understand why he was so adamant about making the changes. I refused to change the dates and told him to complete the report. That is the last I heard of it."

Chuck showed him the report and asked Rick if that was his signature.

"It sure looks like it," he said. Chuck asked him again if he was sure he did not sign it.

Agent Barber said, "I am absolutely sure."

As a result of the wrong date, Agent Duffy went to the United States Attorney's Office and asked the prosecutor to drop the case against Spencer 'Skip' Stone and not embarrass his partner. He told the prosecutor that they would most likely find Stone with a firearm again.

We took the handcuffs off Agent Barber and told him he would not be arrested, and the indictment would be dismissed. Then we told Rick bout Spencer's history, from shooting up FBI homes to being the victim of a homicide in Rockville, Maryland.

He asked us, 'What in the hell is Duffy involved in?'

Chuck said, 'We were hoping you could tell us.'

Rick replied, 'The only thing I know is that for the last six to eight weeks, he has been acting strange with a lot of mood swings and strange conversations. It got so bad that I started documenting it thinking he was having a mental breakdown and needed help. The last eight to ten days have been his worst.

I asked him, 'Where is that documentation now.'

Rick said, 'Home in my desk drawer.'

'How did you get here this morning?' I asked.

'I drove my Bureau car and Jim rode with me.' He told me.

Chuck explained to Rick that an evidence technician would go to his home with him, and Rick was to open his desk drawer and point to the documents. The technician will take photos and then take the documentation as evidence.

We asked Rick one more question, 'Are you willing to give testimony to the grand jury and testify against Agent Duffy if needed?

'Can you tell me how serious this is?' Rick asked.

I answered, 'Let me put it this way. If he is convicted, and I am quite sure he will be, he will spend the remainder of his life behind bars.'

And that was when Rick asked, 'When do you want me to testify?"

"If anything is worthy of a man's best and hardest effort, that thing is the utterance of what he believes to be the truth."
—Edwin Arlington Robinson

CHAPTER 31

After our 2:00 p.m. Zoom meeting, I had a conference call with Steve, Bill Rounds and Janice Buckley regarding the press release. Bill brought everyone up to date and to say it was out of control was an understatement. There were now foreign radio and televisions stations making predictions on the future of America, and it was not good news for the President.

I told everyone that this may be working to our advantage. The stock market would be closing in less than an hour and it was only down by fifteen percent. And with the weekend coming, my recommendation was that we do not release anything today and they all agreed. I said I would call Jim and talk to him and unless I called them back, we would release nothing until Monday afternoon.

I called Jim and gave him the latest, adding "The foreign press is blaming this on the weakness and the corruption of our

President and the corruption in the Department of Justice. And the press is saying there will be at least one hundred or so arrests next week, which we know is impossible especially since we have not examined any of the evidence that was seized today. One of our most powerful weapons, paranoia is working for us."

And Jim said, "Yes, it is. The paranoia in the White House, the Justice Department and the 'deep state' must be at the highest levels possible. I agree that we should wait until Monday.

But now we have a larger problem. We have no idea who is in charge at the Attorney General's Office or the FBI. And uncontrolled paranoia could result in desperation and a violent retaliation. I want everyone in our group, including Tony, and their families to be packed and ready to be picked up or on the way to the lodge in thirty minutes and that includes Tom, Sharon, and Jason. I will send a text now. In fear that this could happen, I called Ben and Carol Thursday evening and they are ready for us. I will pick you up and we can talk on the way."

I hung up the phone and to be honest, I did not think it would come to this. Thank the Lord that Jim had the foresight to be prepared.

A WATCH24 agent and Jim picked me up, and on our way, Jim completed our earlier conversation .

Jim explained, "I did not want to take the time to explain everything to you earlier so here is the rest of the story. Mark Lawton and Bill Holland and his family are also heading for the lodge. FBI Agent Richard Barber is at the safe house to help protect Dave Wilcox and Janice, and I have enough WATCH24 agents there to make sure they are all safe. I also have two WATCH24 agents in a car watching each of our homes.

There is so much confusion in Washington and such a wide split in Congress, that I asked Judge Waters if we could get an emergency order to appoint George to acting FBI Director and Tom to acting Attorney General. We have a growing support from Congress and that may help."

By 8:30 p.m., everyone was at the lodge, and Kim and Patricia announced that dinner would be served at nine. This is the first time that our group of eight and our families have been together. And just knowing that we were all safe gave me a level of comfort.

The meal was wonderful and everyone appeared relaxed. Not surprisingly, Kim was enjoying every minute of it and was thrilled that Joe and Ann Smith were sitting together.

After dinner, we had our dessert sitting in front of the large screen television, watching the news channel. Our four arrests had grown to be the only news. They started to create subtitles that they thought would explain what was going on:

"America In Danger"

"A Government in Turmoil"

"The US President in Fear of His Life"

"President Ignores Emergency"

"What is Going on in America"

These are fitting examples of the press making up exaggerated stories when they have no news or news they do not like. An honest press would have reported a story like this:

"We are hearing rumors from 'unknown sources' that four officials from the Justice Department have been arrested, arraigned and incarcerated with no bail currently set. The White House stated that they had no information on the arrests

and referred us to the Attorney General, who has not returned our calls. We will keep you up to date as soon as we learn more details."

When is the last time you read a story like this?

The story that really caught our attention was the lead story on the 11:00 o'clock news:

"The Federal Bureau of Investigation has ordered all sworn FBI personnel to report to their offices immediately."

Now everyone was watching the television. We spent the next hour speculating who was in charge and what their plan could be. At about midnight they announced that:

"unconfirmed sources tell us that the order for all sworn personnel to their offices came from the White House."

An hour later, the news reported:

"all FBI sworn personnel were released to return to their residents."

Those of us that were still in front of the television made several unflattering comments about our federal government and went to bed.

In the morning, we all had a nice breakfast and Kim again noted to me in a whisper that Joe and Ann were sitting together. I once heard that happily married women want to see every single friend happily married, so I took that as a compliment and realized that I also would like to see Joe and Ann together.

Jim asked our group to all come into another room so we could have a meeting. Jim also invited Tom, Sharon, Mark, Bill, Carol and Ben to join us.

Jim stated, "I have good news. We had no problems last night and everything went smoothly. But George has even better news. Go ahead, George."

"We all had a dream come true very early this morning," George stated. "Remember last night when the 11 p.m. news reported that all the sworn FBI agents were ordered to report to their offices and then released an hour later to return to their homes. Evidently, that wasn't quite true.

Yesterday's early morning arrests spread like a wildfire through the Field Offices and the agents had a preplanned action plan in place. They all reported as ordered last night, but secretly recorded most, if not all, of the meetings. When the supervisors gave out assignments that would have violated their oath of office, they refused the assignment and went home. That news also spread like a wildfire through the Field Offices, and all the agents left and went home. Today at noon there will be many agents and supervisors with two lawyers from a Washington, DC firm, making a public statement in front of the Justice Building, stating that the rank and file of the FBI no longer has any confidence in the Director of the FBI, the office of the Attorney General, the Vice President and the President of the United States. They are demanding they be removed from office and are ready to file affidavits with the acting Attorney General that contain the evidence outlining the felonies they have committed, to include treason."

Everyone applauded.

Jim said, "Our work has just gotten a hell of a lot easier. Let's watch the news at noon, have a nice lunch together, and then head back home to finish our work. Next Friday we will do an evaluation and with safety precautions in place, we may allow everyone to decide to go home or stay a few more days."

The noon press conference shocked the world. With the worldwide coverage, I am not sure how much longer the President and Vice President could remain in office. The follow-up news stories should be interesting.

We had another wonderful meal and I could tell that Kim and Marie were ready to go home. Jason was surprised by how nice the accommodations were and was pleased that he could also stay until Friday.

On the way home, Jim was saying how pleased he was that everyone enjoyed the lodge.

I added, "We do not have to wait to have our life threatened before we use the lodge. Let's develop a schedule to use it two or three times a year just to relax."

"I would like that, Chuck," Jim said. "But we need to bring our entire families."

"Deal," I replied with a grin. "I would like nothing better."

"People think of leaders as men devoted to service, and by service they mean that these men serve their followers. The real leader serves truth, not people."
—J. B. Yeats

CHAPTER 32

I was up early and ready for church. I could not remember a time when I was any more thankful for God's guidance than I was today. He has answered our prayers in so many ways on this case that there is no doubt we were fortunate to witness His Divine Intervention. There is power in prayer.

Knowing Kim could be home by Friday motivated me to clean the house and that's just what I did. However, I did take the occasional break just to take a quick look at the latest news.

At dinner time, I opened the freezer and there it was, the last frozen dinner that Kim had prepared for me before she had to leave. I thought about cooking dinner for myself tonight but before I realized what I had done, the meal was spinning on the turntable in the microwave.

After dinner, I went to my desk to prepare for tomorrow's

Zoom meeting. I did not have anything regarding the case, but an article I read in the Sunday paper deserved at least a mention, so I wrote it up.

I have not been able to get caught up on my sleep from Friday night, so I started a load of my laundry and went to bed a little early.

The Monday morning Zoom meeting started with Jim saying, "Look at the progress we have made since last Thursday's Zoom meeting. We are beginning to see the light at the end of the tunnel. I give all of you and God the credit. You should be proud of your service to the country we all love dearly.

The media is out of control and getting worse every minute. Bill and Janice, our media consultants, are attempting to stay on top of it. Right now, they want us to remain silent and will call me at noon with an update."

"Tom, you are up first for an update on the Rockville homicide."

Tom said, "I called Detective Tim Preston at the Rockville Police Department and told him that FBI Agent James Duffy shot and killed Skip Spencer at the request of Assistant Attorney General John Williams and both have been indicted and arrested on unrelated charges and are in jail with no bail."

There was a brief pause before Detective Preston replied, "You have got to be kidding me!"

I said, 'I wish I were,' and explained the story to him. He was in shock.

I told him our investigation is continuing and it appears that Agent Duffy will be cooperating. We will see if we can recover the weapon and asked him to give us a few days and Steve Mason, the Special Prosecutor, will call the Rockville State's Attorney and arrange for him to speak to Duffy."

General Monroe was next. "This is the week that the Department of Defense will eliminate thousands of soldiers in the reserves and the National Guard. Is there anything we can do to stop it?"

Jim replied, "I do not think we can stop it, but I do think there will come a time very soon when they will be reinstated. I hope they know that."

And General Monroe said, "They will. Thank you."

"You're up next, Chuck." Jim stated.

"I only have one item or one question depending on how you look at it," I told everyone.

"In yesterday's paper I read an article where the columnist was trying to justify the President's $86 billion taxpayer bailout for 185 union pension plans. Which by the way, never has to be repaid. In my opinion, this is nothing more than pure, unadulterated corruption and no one says a word about it. The national debt today is $26.7 trillion with an annual interest cost of $479 billion, which is all coming out of our pockets. And here we sit, doing everything we can possibly do to save our country while our corrupt government, with a single signature from a corrupt President, continues to destroy it. We are all willing to die to save America, but unless we make some dramatic changes in how the federal government operates, we are doing nothing but throwing sand against the tide. And my question is, can we find a President who has the courage and stamina to take on this task?"

Judge Walters commented, "And this is why both the President and the Vice President need to be replaced."

Next, Steve gave us an update on the grand jury schedule.

"First let, me tell you how professional and organized the evidence collection process went. The United States Marshals did an outstanding job and the amount of evidence seized far exceeded my expectations.

George, as soon as you get appointed Acting Director, please figure out a way that the laboratory can start helping us analyze the electronic evidence. The sooner we have all emails and phone numbers in our data base, the faster we can uncover the 'deep state.'

The grand jury will start again on Wednesday afternoon and continue through Friday. Next Monday we will have two grand juries seated. Yesterday, Tony and I spent three hours with Jim Duffy and later this morning, we will be sitting down with Dave Wilcox again. It will take us a few days, but our grand jury presentations will be ready in time.

And Tom, we have some information from Duffy on the murder weapon and I will speak to the Rockville District Attorney this afternoon."

Jim spoke again, "I think we are all fully aware that we do not have the resources to fully investigate this case. George and I had a lengthy conversation on Sunday afternoon discussing a strategy to compile a list of sworn FBI agents, supervisors, attorneys and specialists to be assigned to this corruption case. I will let George discuss procedure we will be using."

As George took the floor, he explained, "Jim and I selected a small group of current and retired agents that we believe are honest, have integrity and more than anything else, want to return the Bureau to an agency that can regain the respect of the public. They have already started their assignment to prepare two lists for this group, The first will be those they recommend for the case investigation. The second list will be those that they recommend for investigation by the first group."

Jim concluded the meeting by saying. "As you know, the FBI has been my life, and what we are doing here is giving the Bureau one chance to redeem themselves. We need to give them time to get their act together and if they are not successful, the Federal Bureau of Investigation needs to be abolished."

Sitting and waiting for the 'second shoe to drop' is not something I usually cherish. But today it works for me since I have not finished my house cleaning and I wanted to get groceries and other items in anticipation of Kim's return. It was 7:20 in the morning and absolutely the best time to go to the grocery store. I took my time examining everything before placing it in my cart. To the perfect stranger, I am sure I looked like I knew what I was doing. Obviously, I did not. The total for two bags of groceries was $143.70.

I put the groceries away, filling the new shelf I added to the pantry and sat down to read the paper. Now the media is speculating that the entire federal government will be "restructured." I would not be surprised if one of the Attorney General's cronies slipped the media a copy of their proposed organizational chart.

I went back to my cleaning chores and within five minutes, my phone rang. It was Jim.

I answered, "Hey Jim, what's up?"

"Are you watching the news?" he asked. I responded in the negative told him that I just finished reading the paper."

"The TV news is better." He told me. "They just had a story about the federal agencies being overwhelmed by the unusual number of retirement and resignations this morning.

That's good news, but not why I called you. My favorite Congressman called me and told me to make sure Tom and George have an updated résumé and are prepared to meet with selected congressional leaders either this afternoon or tomorrow morning. I already notified them. Get ready, the pace has picked up. Talk to you later."

That was great news, but I expected some resistance.

For the next two hours, the only rooms that were cleaned had a television.

The shocker came at 2:00 p.m. with a press release from the White House. Evidently, the Vice President has had enough humiliation and has resigned due to a medical condition effective Friday. I doubt we will ever know the true reason she resigned, but I will not look a gift horse in the mouth.

The second part of the press release was naming retired Admiral Matthew Thomas as the President's choice to fill the vacancy left by the Vice President's resignation and asking that the Senate will approve it as soon as possible. That shocked me. I know he and the President spent a lot of time together, years ago, on the train going back and forth from home to Washington. But Admiral Thomas is a known conservative that has never belonged to a political party. Perhaps this was the compromise which will allow the President to maintain some sort of dignity until his term ends and allow Thomas to be the decision maker and put this country back on track. If this is true, someone in Washington has made a brilliant decision, which is infrequent and highly unusual.

It did not take long for the media to switch their top story from a corrupt federal government to the unknown savior of America. For our group this was much better than we expected.

Jim immediately sent a text saying this was great news and he would try and get full confirmation for George and Tom at the same time, stating that Admiral Thomas would not be able to make any progress without an Attorney General and FBI Director. I took this to mean they would not be "Acting" which would require a second Senate confirmation.

Our prediction was accurate, the pace picked up speed.

On Tuesday, the weapon that killed Skip Spencer was recovered and the Rockville State's Attorney planned to indict Duffy and Williams early next week.

On Wednesday and Thursday, the grand jury handed down six additional indictments.

On Wednesday, over 5,000 names, numbers and email addresses were added to our 'deep state' data base. Also added to the data base was all the White House visitors log for the last 18 months.

On Thursday, George and Tom met with congressional leaders and had a meeting with Admiral Thomas which they said was very promising.

On Friday, the six indicted people were arrested early in the morning and committed with no bail.

On Friday morning, the Senate confirmed Admiral Thomas as the next Vice President of the United States, Thomas Wilson as the next United States Attorney General and George Peters as the new Director of the Federal Bureau of Investigation with a ten-year term.

On Friday at 4:00 p.m., all three of them would be given their oath of office by the Chief Justice, effective 12:01 a.m. on Saturday.

Jim made sure their families would be present for the ceremony. However, he suggested that the presence of our full group would raise questions from the media and may put a cloud over the ceremony. I agreed.

At about 3:00 p.m., Kim, Marie, Jason and Katherine came through the door. It was great to see them home. They noticed the "WELCOME HOME" cake on the kitchen counter next to the flowers and Kim thanked me with a kiss and tears in her eyes.

I announced that Tom and Sharon would be here at four with dinner from Olive Garden.

Kim replied, "I know. I called and asked him to do the same and he told me, 'Too late, Dad is one step ahead of you."

And everyone laughed.

"The open mind never acts; when we have done our utmost to arrive at a reasonable conclusion, we still, when we can reason and investigate no more, must close our minds for the moment with a snap, and act dogmatically on our conclusions."
—George Bernard Shaw

EPILOGUE

With a new Vice President, Tom and George in their new positions, and the growing corps of incorruptible FBI agents, our group's work has been completed. This investigation will last for several months before all the players, from the upper echelon of the Justice Department to the "deep state" civil servants, are brought to justice.

I doubt that the President will remain in office for very long; first because of his health and secondly because I know Tom will move the corruption case involving the President's son, to the top of the pile. And I find comfort knowing that Vice President Thomas will be the next President.

The missing dirty bombs have always troubled me. I trust that George will do everything within his power to locate them if they still exist or ever existed. It has been thirteen years and they have never surfaced. That's a plus. As they age and continue to deteriorate, their power decreases until they become useless.

There are several more important updates that are relevant.

Both Mark Lawton and David Wilcox are excited with their new positions as WATCH24 agents.

Joe and Ann are engaged and are planning a fall wedding with a honeymoon in Hawaii.

Marie and Jason are proud parents of John Charles weighing in at just over 7 pounds.

And finally, Tom and Sharon are going to make us grandparents again. I knew it!

END

MEET THE AUTHOR

CARL BAKER IS A VETERAN &
SENIOR LAW ENFORCEMENT OFFICER

Carl Baker retired after 40 years in law enforcement and public safety. He served as a Colonel in both the New York State Police and the Virginia State Police, as Deputy Secretary of Public Safety to Virginia Governor George Allen, and as Chief of Police for Chesterfield County, VA. After retiring, he operated his own public safety consulting firm and was a Partner in Decide Smart, LLC. Carl is also a veteran of the U. S. Army, having served in both the Engineer Corps and Military Police Corps. A native of New York State, Carl and his wife, Katherine, now reside in The Villages, Florida.

YOUR NEXT GREAT
READ FROM
CARL R. BAKER
AND "THE DC SEVEN."

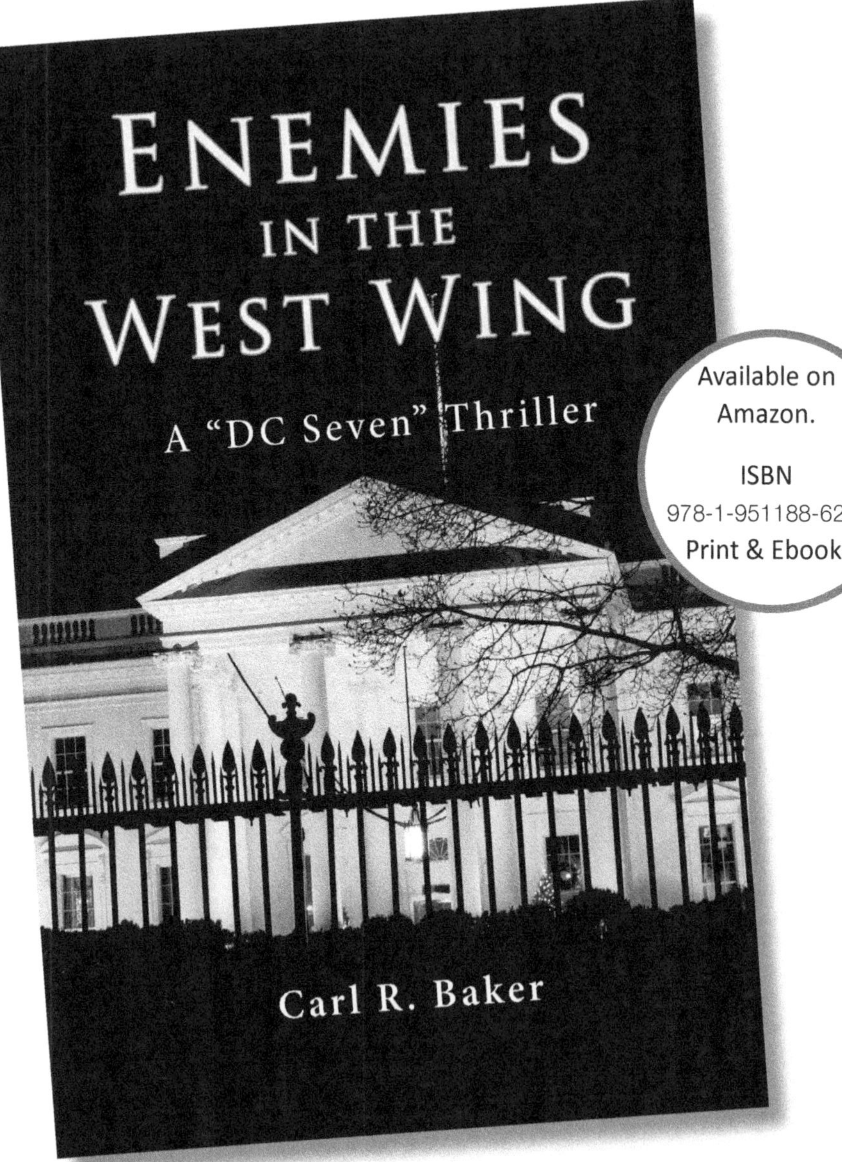

The President of the United States has gone rogue!

The first book in the "DC Seven" Thriller series.

With the Nation in grave peril, seven resolute patriots lead a team of security and law enforcement professionals with the self-appointed mission of saving their country—placing themselves and their families in great danger.

Quiet, highly effective and experienced leaders, they call themselves "The DC Seven." A retired Deputy Director of the FBI, a Special Agent in Charge of the White House Secret Service, a retired four-star General, a retired Supreme Court Judge, a former United States Attorney, a retired CIA Analyst/Technician, and the Deputy Director of the FBI made seven.

Murder, a car bombing, and home invasions tell them the President is deadly serious, and they believe, he has access to radioactive "dirty bombs." But preventing the President from fundamentally changing America will be much more difficult and tragic than they had ever realized.

www.ingramcontent.com/pod-product-compliance
Lightning Source LLC
Chambersburg PA
CBHW070452200726
48293CB00007B/2171